WEAVER

Maria Zaman

WEAVER

Vanguard Press

A CIP catalogue record for this title is
available from the British Library.

ISBN 978-1-80016-383 6

*Vanguard Press is an imprint of
Pegasus Elliot MacKenzie Publishers Ltd.*
www.pegasuspublishers.com

First Published in 2022

**Vanguard Press
Sheraton House Castle Park
Cambridge England**
Printed & Bound in Great Britain

Acknowledgements

Thank you to all at Pegasus Elliot Mackenzie Publishers for their hard work and diligence regarding the fine tuning of my manuscript preparatory to publication. And not forgetting all those who contributed behind the scenes to breathe life into this project. And finally, thanks goes out to Pixabay from where the cover image was originally sourced.

1

Welcome back, faithful reader, my silent, resolute companion. I'm glad you found the time to rejoin me and the rest of the Pariahs during this — how shall I put it? — pivotal moment in humankind's history; I think that's an accurate surmise, as I'm sure you're very aware. How could you not be with the constant twenty-four-hour news coverage broadcasting the return of Maria and her entourage? At the last count, the total global figure of Nephilim was just over six thousand, so I think it's fair to describe this visitation as a full-scale invasion. Don't you? And no doubt, like the billions of others tuned in, you've been transfixed by the images beamed across every terrestrial channel across the globe, waiting with bated breath and chewed fingernails. But the big question that's on everybody's lips is why? What exactly do these visitors want exactly?

Hell, I wish I could enlighten you, but at the moment, my fellow Pariahs and I are somewhat stumped. Well, not entirely. Old memories have been resurfacing of late, you see. Like ancient, dusty veils being drawn aside to reveal something long forgotten and lain hidden, quite literally, in plain sight for aeons.

And I mean, this goes way back. But we're still piecing things together. So, if you'll indulge me once more, I will share these revelations with you as and when we become conversant with them ourselves. But first, perhaps something less replete with 'impending doom'. A big sonorous, echoey voice would be quite appropriate right about now.

But events preceding this unforeseen invasion, regarding ourselves, have been pretty sweet, except for the emergence of a remnant connected to our previous exploits, which necessitated a trip to Cambodia. Which, if I remember, and have the time, I will later relate to you. But for now, I think we have enough to contend with. So, two album releases under our belts, a Stateside and European tour successfully concluded, and two marriages — yes, plural!

So, make yourself comfortable and try to forget Maria and her entourage for now, hard as I know that's going to be, and I'll bring you up-to-date with regards to the Pariahs. Incidentally, so you can picture the scene for yourself, we have stepped through a portal and lodged ourselves in my New York apartment. I sold my London pad after the military ransacked the place shortly after we had successfully, or so we thought, dealt with Maria. The place felt violated; it no longer felt like my own any more. And as the military are quite aware of our Canadian residence, I thought my New York apartment to be by far the safest prospect — I hope. Although from the window here, I can just make

8

out that the Nephilim have stationed a representative of their race smack in the middle of Central Park. Which is something I can't quite convince myself is purely coincidental. Periodically, you can just make out her metallic crimson armour glinting in the fading sunlight amongst the density of greenery.

As you will have noticed for yourself, they are quite the rainbow warrior elite on this occasion. Whether it's some form of military denomination amongst their kind or just a fashion statement, who knows? But she's certainly drawing a crowd. Even the streets surrounding this green haven within this bustling metropolis are rapidly filling with vehicles and inquisitive pedestrians. The police in attendance will soon be overwhelmed as the crowd swells, and they have already called upon the assistance of the military in an attempt to control the crowd. I can just make out the first military entourage arriving now. But if everyone had gained access to some of the images we've been party to, then these curious sightseers would be maintaining a respectful distance. Perhaps even rushing home and nailing crooked pieces of wood across doors and windows. And how did we access these images that have been withheld from the public? Well, that's pretty much down to Maddie, who has revealed a remarkable talent for computer hacking over the last few months. Where and how she developed this skill is a complete mystery to me. The hows and whys aside, she has infiltrated several restricted systems, and to date, one military satellite with the same ease one would log into Amazon and peruse the items for sale there.

But anyway, I'm getting ahead of myself; all will be revealed in good time, including, hopefully, a solution to this alien invasion. Although I use the term 'alien', the Nephilim are perhaps not technically what most people would deem as alien. Long gone are the little green men, replaced by little greys with big dark eyes, you know the kind of thing. But in some respects, they probably are, alien, that is.

It's complicated.

So, where to begin...

2

Since our big reveal some time ago now, we've recorded and released two discs. Three technically, but this untimely arrival by the Nephilim has curtailed any immediate release we had entertained — perhaps permanently!

As I mentioned, two tours were staged following each release, as I'm sure you're aware. Maybe you were even there in person? In which case, thank you for your support, and I hope you enjoyed the show.

Deek, as promised, was behind the wheel of our very luxurious bus for most of the tour. 'Bus' actually seems hardly adequate to accurately describe it, to be honest, and I don't know how Deek managed to navigate some of the roads successfully without scraping the paintwork or pancaking pedestrians. But still, I felt stifled inside this luxury apartment on wheels at times with us all packed in. And far too much of our time, whilst being ferried between venues, was spent immersing ourselves within the Marvel universe.

I wish now that I'd never introduced them to the *Avengers* as the arguments it instigated, regarding who could takedown which superhero, began to grate on me very quickly. If I hear the line: 'I could take the green one with one hand tied behind my back' one more time…

And bizarrely, the line between fact and fantasy is still somewhat hazy within the group, as I discovered after having been drawn into a rather lengthy discussion regarding Hugh Jackman's memorable portrayal of Wolverine. Yes, I foolishly introduced them to the X-Men as well. Wolverine, unsurprisingly, being a particular favourite of Mist's.

'I would very much like to meet this Wolverine,' she confessed to me one day whilst re-watching *Logan*.

So would I, Mist! Don't tell J I said that (that's Jackson, more on that later). Anyway, I thought the visceral violence would appeal to her in particular.

'You do realise that this film is fictitious?'

'Of course, I am no fool.'

But despite this, she still believed that the character himself was, in actuality, very real, and she approached me, later on, to enquire if we could contact him and find out where exactly he had had his eponymous metal claws surgically implanted.

I know! Unbelievable, right? And then the very next day, Kal caught me on my own and asked me the very same thing!

I'm sure they intentionally wind each other up as Kal has a firmer grasp on reality than some of the others do, just to pass the time and amuse themselves. And Sophia, in particular, for an angelic being, has a wicked sense of humour, and I'm sure it was her who had encouraged Kal on that particular occasion.

There was another incident, initiated by Sophia, which necessitated me becoming involved as I had to convince Nikki that the rhino she had adopted at San Diego Zoo was not available for her to now collect and take home with her. I've no idea what she intended on doing with it — take it on tour with us? It wouldn't have surprised me, as they've very much embraced the epitome of touring as part of a rock band.

Don't get me wrong, I have to confess I had a good laugh about that one myself, but I felt things were starting to get a little bit out of hand. Particularly after Deek — I'm shaking a metaphorical fist at you — showed them an interview with a popular rock band from the seventies revealing all the 'high jinks' they got up to whilst on tour. I know 'high jinks' may be a little understating what then occurred, but I'm sure Maddie, Nikki and Deek merely viewed it as a little boisterous fun with which to pass the time.

The main incident in question being the launching of a seventy-inch television out of a hotel window in an attempt to emulate the antics of this rock band.

In between long periods spent on the road, we did feel the need for the occasional luxurious pit stop with ensuite — heaven!

Anyway, rather disappointed by the result of modern technology impacting solid concrete, the three of them managed to secure a forty-inch old-school cathode-ray tube television. The bomb-like detonation was much more to their liking. Fortunately, I intervened at this point before they could appropriate more. Still, no one was charged — or worse — locked up. But I would have to take my hat off (not that I wear one) to any officer who was willing to even attempt locking up either Maddie or Nikki.

I've barely mentioned J, he'll be feeling left out, so I'd better rectify that. It turns out that Jackson is his Christian name. I'd always presumed that that was his surname. Full title, Jackson Emerson Miller, J to me. We got hitched in Las Vegas together with Mist and Anastassia — the terrible twins! Between you and me, they remind me of those spooky twin girls in *The Shining*, but grown-up and one of them has gone a bit Goth. I've got to confess it was the best day ever, and we took a couple of days out of our heavy schedule to… well, you know, chill out before hitting the road again.

I know, Vegas! A bit clichéd and tacky. But we thought, why wait? Everybody I would have wanted to attend my marriage was in attendance, so it was the perfect opportunity. And just for the record, the ceremony wasn't sanctioned by an Elvis impersonator. But after viewing the array of famous personas willing to wed us in holy matrimony, Mist approached me, and I said no immediately before she even uttered a word. I just knew what was coming, and there was just no way Wolverine was going to perform the ceremony. Even if he was available.

Ix, throughout the whole tour, just took everything in her stride. The introspective soul that she is, she just seemed to magically appear where and when she was needed to offer advice and calm my nerves. I think I would've pulled my hair out if she hadn't been on board the crazy coach.

The concerts themselves proved to be a huge success. We played to capacity; every ticket snapped up in minutes after being made available.

I spent much of the set enjoying the performance with J from the wings, only making an appearance for a handful of songs, stepping directly on stage through a hastily conjured portal to rapturous applause. I still find it very intimidating standing up there in front of thousands of madly screaming fans, but the rest of the band thrived on it.

The American leg of our tour complete, we then took a short break to complete our second album before taking on Europe, with the full intention of bringing our unique blend of rock and blues to the rest of the world in the foreseeable future. But now...

This leg of our tour was equally auspicious but perhaps a little more subdued, which I put down to the weather as it was fast approaching autumn, and it rained... a lot.

As we had promised Deek, we played to yet another sold-out show in Glasgow. Deek then took Kal, Maddie (Mads as he now refers to her) and Nikki into Glasgow city centre afterwards for a proper Scottish night out!

I still don't know what transpired, but at least it didn't make the news, and for that, I should be thankful. They returned at four in the morning, Kal carrying an unconscious Deek under one arm, Maddie and Nikki in tow, singing bawdy football chants with no concept of what the words actually pertained to and no doubt learnt from Deek.

It wasn't until we'd done dates across the UK, Scandinavia, Belgium, the Netherlands and headed south into France and Spain that the weather finally improved. But a dark cloud was soon to cast its shadow over us, one which has never entirely dissipated.

During our many months on the road, Nikki obviously had to 'sustain' herself periodically. And one night whilst in… you know what, it's probably best I don't disclose that kind of incriminating evidence, it's best you don't know. Long story short, she got careless one night. After siphoning off her latest victim — I still shudder when I think about it — she disposed of the body. 'A worthless rapist scumbag,' as she succinctly put it. No great loss to society then. But this 'worthless rapist scumbag' happened to be the son of a regarded and rather influential local politician, and consequently, a full-scale manhunt was launched after he had been reported missing. And despite Nikki having 'dismantled' — yes, that's exactly how she worded it — her leftovers and discarded the parts, an arm turned up. Hooked by a young fisherman whilst on a camping trip with his father. Not what they had in mind to grill over their campfire that night, I'm quite sure. And said arm sported a tattoo which was immediately identified.

No other remains were located, yet, and the arm has mysteriously disappeared from police custody. I wonder how on earth that could have happened? But the incident haunts me, and after that event, I don't know whether it was paranoia or if those placard bearing fire-and-brimstone types were always there in force outside the venues we were scheduled to play at. Their slogans advised fans to boycott our gigs or be faced with fiery damnation or words to that effect. But the fans were merely amused by their presence, and I'm sure that they were always in attendance, but at the same time, I'm quite convinced their movement has increased in size and fanaticism. Waving crucifixes! Unbelievable, I don't know whether they were an attempt to ward us off or an encouragement for Sophia to sign them. The hand-painted placards displayed numerous slogans of a similar theme: *Satan's consorts; you will burn in hell; repent.* How very sadly misinformed they were. Satan doesn't exist, neither does hell for that matter and repent what? And to whom exactly? And where do these people come from? A village somewhere in the sixteenth century? And bizarrely, one placard I noticed, the red heart is what caught my eye, displayed the message: *I luv u Nikki.*

I suppose it was all part of being in a rock band, something generations of musicians have had to endure for decades. But since the tattooed arm incident, I can't help worrying about other evidence of her dietary needs turning up in the future. And to be fair to Nikki, she does only target individuals that anyone with a degree of acumen would still see as parasites who merely preyed on the weak and vulnerable. She was doing society a favour.

But in complete contrast to our placard-wielding anti-fans, we have gathered a religious fan base as well who turn up to gigs in a state of pious fervour. Literally swooning at the sight of Sophia as she sweeps above the upstretched arms. Religion has taken a very hard knock of late, particularly since Sophia spread her divine wings and took to the air all those months previously. She could start a new religion all by herself. I've even spotted the occasional squadron of nuns amongst the headbangers and hippies. Yes, hippies do still exist; I've seen them for myself, but I think they're very timid and only come out at night. Unless these nuns were actually fetishists, of course? You know, that never occurred to me until now.

On the whole, it's been a wild ride and vastly enjoyable. I'm not sure the locals will welcome us back with open arms in some places though… there was that strange place in Slovakia. When with much chanting and encouragement from fans after the show, Kal, with a little help from Nikki, tore a police car in half.

Now that's rock 'n' roll!

Now I'm getting to the more serious matter of the Nephilim. It was during the final couple of weeks of the

European tour, as we were winding down, that the dreams began. I've always suffered from vivid, and on occasion, disturbing dreams, but these were in a league all of their own.

I attempted to keep this new development to myself until we at least made it back home to Canada. Back to the solitude, fresh air and peace, I can't tell you how much, at this stage, I was looking forward to getting back. But J being intimately connected to me — hey, I'm talking psychically! — and considering the powers the rest of the crew are endowed with made secrecy an impossible task. And concurrently, unbeknown to me at the time, all the others were experiencing similar conceptions. Long dormant memories resurfacing, regardless of their conscious state. Images flashing into existence revealing details of something we had all forgotten.

Looking back now, I realise that these memories had, in fact, been concealed, painted over so professionally that none of us had been aware of their presence, and I was the one who was being specifically targeted. I think the others were experiencing this as mnemonics, collaterally, so to speak, directly from me and probably enhanced by J's unique psychic abilities.

But why me? It didn't take me long to figure that one out; it was because of my relationship with magic. I can almost see a religious zealot waving a placard with *Devilry* printed on it in front of the window. No mean feat as we're on the seventeenth floor! This was something the others didn't have direct access to, their talents the result of inherent abilities. Even J's skills are based more on psychic projections than magical conjurations. And until that epiphanic moment, I'd never given the true source of my powers that much thought. I'd always just presumed that it was like aether that I plucked and harnessed from a plane of existence that ran concurrently with our own. Something I dipped into like sipping from a cup. But I suppose with all such natural elements, they all have to spring from somewhere. And in this particular case, this source had a name.

This revelation didn't hit me until we were settled once more back in my log cabin in Canada. And I say hit me, I mean like a shovel to the back of the head! But minus the concussion.

We had only been back two days, Deek having taken the opportunity to go home to Glasgow to visit family, when I sat bolt upright in bed in the early hours that morning, wide awake, called back from a deep, vivid and rather disturbing dream. The name of our, until now, forgotten ninth member of our team on my lips.

Nephthys.

3

This naming coincided, or perhaps prompted, an anamnesis amongst us Pariahs.

Now here's a perfect opportunity to maintain my responsibility in trying to introduce at least one new word into your vocabulary per day. Unless, of course, your literary knowledge far surpasses my own.

Anamnesis — which means a remembrance, and in particular, regarding memories of a previous existence. Which in our case is so spookily accurate, as you will soon come to realise.

It was as if a room had been opened up in a house that I'd lived in all my lives. A room that I had always known had existed but had somehow overlooked. And now that that room had been unlocked and the door had been thrown open, I found it inconceivable that I'd overlooked it all these years. I say years, but in actuality, it had been centuries. This stems back to our very inception. Nephthys was an original and integral part of the team. As Kal put it, our ennead was complete.

I'm spoiling you now, two new words in such close succession!

Ennead — a group or set of nine and was something very prevalent in Ancient Egypt, where I believe the term was first coined and where the Pariahs first came into being. Although that is a title that we only recently conceived and utilised in the naming of our band.

Okay, I hope you're still with me, my patient friend, as I'll now explain in more detail why this inexplicable event had suddenly burgeoned and why Nephthys had finally decided to reach out and re-establish contact after so many centuries. Although, in retrospect, it now seems obvious that it was in response to the arrival of the Nephilim on our shores. Or, to be more accurate, an augural event, as the first dreams I'd experienced occurred one full moon cycle before the invasion fleet arrived.

I'll relate the details as they became apparent to myself and the rest of my crew, although if you'll allow me a little literary licence as the arrival of the Nephilim, which at the time even *we* hadn't anticipated, has certainly cast new light on the situation, and consequently we have now gained a clearer insight into the matter. Or, at least, confirmed what we had previously speculated and suspected.

So, I've mixed past and present details up a little before and after the arrival of who I mistakenly presumed to be our Maria at our Glastonbury gig, which took place two weeks after our arrival back in Canada, so you can better understand, hopefully. Headlining on the famous pyramid stage — I wonder now if that, in itself, was a prophetic occurrence — I can still barely believe that we had been invited to participate in that world acclaimed music event.

So, despite the recent revelations, we still had to prepare for this momentous occasion in the band's progress, a significant milestone in our careers, to say the least.

We picked up Deek the day before the gig — Alice-style — and portaled directly to the venue. Our road crew arrived by more conventional means. If you didn't attend, then I'm sure you caught some of our act, as it was televised live, which now also included the arrival of a Nephilim, materialising amidst the crowd during our encore to a tumultuous roar from the audience. I think that they were so caught up in the moment that many just presumed that her arrival was just some aspect of the elaborate stage show we presented.

Anyway, backtracking a little, I'll share with you what we knew then and what we know now. But keep this information under your hat, so to speak. Or if you don't wear a hat, then in a box under your bed or at the back of a cupboard, because if this leaks and the authorities get a whiff before we can formulate some sort of cohesive plan, then... well, the military are going to be all over us like wasps on a sticky bun.

I hope I can rely on your discretion. Right then, good.

Firstly, there are still some glaringly obvious gaping holes in our knowledge which I hope will be filled in due course. But perhaps I should begin by explaining who Nephthys is in case you're not conversant in Egyptian mythology. She was, and at the moment we can only presume still is, a goddess associated with several aspects of Egyptian life, but the one I most resonate with is magic. This is why I have a direct line to her subconscious and was the obvious point of first contact.

The conversation we shared the morning of my utterance is as accurate as I can recall. I was still a little stunned by the revelation, and I hadn't had my breakfast yet!

When J and I made an appearance, the rest of the Pariahs, Anastassia included, were in attendance and awaiting our arrival in the living room. Ix was standing on the porch just outside the back door staring up to the heavens, which at the time I thought to be rather portentous. Maddie and Nikki were playing the Xbox, arguing over a game they were involved in, bickering like children.

'My warrior is by no means a reflection of my prowess in battle,' Nikki proclaimed. 'This controller is defective.'

There's nothing wrong with the controller.

'It is your gaming technique that is flawed,' Maddie countered.

And so on; they do it all the time.

Mist and Anastassia were seated together, hand in prosthetic hand, patiently awaiting my arrival, while Kal was drumming agitatedly on my coffee (tea) table.

I'm going to drop 'coffee' from now on and hope that tea table catches on. This is something Kal does a lot of now. It's a rare sight to see her without at least one pair of drumsticks in motion.

'Where's Sophia?' I ask, noting our resident angel is missing.

Kal just points behind me with a drumstick and carries on tapping out a rhythm without missing a beat.

I turn around, and Sophia presents me with a cup of steaming tea as she exits the kitchen, her other hand firmly clutching a tub of Ben & Jerry's.

'For breakfast?' I ask, gratefully accepting the mug.

'You know my sugar levels drop when I'm stressed.'

A likely excuse. Seraphim suffering from stress and sugar crashes.

'Then you know?' I ask, mildly surprised, but not much.

Even Maddie and Nikki have curtailed their gaming rivalry for now and have turned to face me. This is when I first heard Kal refer to the ennead — the group of nine.

'Huh!' I distinctly remember saying that at the time on hearing her announcement — not very creative, I know, but I was still a bit sleepy.

'Perhaps you should share with us the details of your dream?' Nikki asks, one perfect eyebrow raised.

How the hell does she look so perfect in the morning? My hair always looks like I've had raccoons rummaging through it!

I just nod and take a seat cradling my mug of tea, and J squeezes in next to me after taking delivery of a mug of coffee retrieved from the kitchen by Sophia, sweeping in and out of the kitchen with all the grace of a ballet dancer and handing it over with a radiant smile. I take a sip of tea and feel better already. Prepared just how I like it and served by an angelic being — it doesn't get much better than that!

'Black, two sugars,' she informs J with a smile that could melt hearts and instigate world peace overnight.

If I didn't know her or was the jealous type, I'd give her a damn good scowl for smiling at my husband like that.

J just raises his eyebrows at me, above his steaming mug, in genuine innocence as he takes a sip of his black coffee.

I snuggle up close to J; I need the contact after the night I've had. And for the record, we don't need direct physical contact to amalgamate and bolster our skills now — I just like the contact. But the addition of a very special pair of wedding rings, crafted by Maddie, certainly helps. A marriage of silver and gold — I don't want to know where she sourced the materials — engraved with ancient and powerful protection charms supplied by Nikki. They're quite beautiful and very potent. A similar pair was created for Mist and Anastassia, but runic symbols were incorporated into the design.

Ix breaks out of her reverie and comes to join the gathering but leaves the door ajar, and I appreciate the cool air as it percolates through the room.

'I presume Alice has shared with you the details of her revelation?' Maddie enquires of J, her gold-tinted shades flashing in the morning light as she turns her head.

He taps the side of his head as he sips before answering. 'Unavoidable side-effect of my abilities. We share dreams quite often. But this one was different,' he ponders. 'It was like overhearing one side of a phone call.' He tries to explain. 'And Alice was at the receiving end, but I could feel the presence of the caller, and she was powerful and somehow familiar.'

'The question is,' says Sophia, taking a seat and crossing her legs underneath her in one smooth action, 'why weren't any of us aware of this ninth person until just recently? I mean, not even God could have been aware of her existence as there were only eight cells prepared in that place.' She pulls a face as she recalls that nightmarish prison, her tub of breakfast ice cream now lying forgotten on my *tea* table.

She makes a good point; I hadn't considered that detail until now. I also sense that she is a little put out and concerned by the fact that she wasn't aware of Nephthys' apparent membership to our team. Let's be honest here, I'm in the presence of divine beings and goddesses, and someone managed to remain hidden from us all and wipe our memories of all knowledge of

27

her existence. Now that's some feat. It would be like pulling a trick over on Derren Brown — who, by the way, has become the focus of much attentive viewing by most here in attendance. That 'tricky-one' as Nikki likes to call him 'would fail to confound me'.

I have my doubts — he's pretty good.

Ix and Kal aside, both of whom haven't been hypnotised by the allure of television. Kal can certainly take it or leave it and can be found more often than not, in between drumming, that is, reading a book, usually something that deserves the raising of an eyebrow or two. I asked her one day what she was reading, and she held it up so I could read the cover: *Quantum Shamanism.* That was a two eyebrower!

And Ix spends a lot of her spare time, most of it, in fact, wandering the forest like some disincarnate spirit. She would scare the hell out of any hikers that happened to be in the vicinity, that's for sure.

Sorry, back to the discussion.

'Because she deemed it necessary to mask her presence, her very existence.'

I nod in response to Nikki's comment, as that's exactly the conclusion I had come to. 'Her name is Nephthys,' I add, but I suspect at least some of those present are aware of this already.

Nikki nods knowingly. 'As I suspected.'

'You did not,' Maddie admonishes.

Nikki just glares back at her, her pupils flaring red, and I'm tempted to send them both to their rooms. I don't know whose look unnerves me more when they're riled. But they do this a lot — it means nothing. I'm sure they even enjoy these clashes between them when they haven't got mortals close at hand to intimidate instead.

'She seeks assistance.' Ix finally enters the conversation. 'She is reaching out, calling to her ennead.'

'That's the feeling I've been getting,' I agree.

'Assistance with what though?' Sophia asks.

I shake my head. 'I don't know,' I answer honestly. 'The images I've been receiving are far from coherent, but...' I take a sip of my tea as I try to organise my thoughts.

'But whatever it's concerning, I can sense that it's not far in the future,' J finishes for me. 'I can feel it like a pressure at the back of my head.'

And I don't think he means far away as in it's-Christmas-in-two-weeks-kind-of-exciting-can-hardly-wait far away. I think he means more if you've got any unfinished business you want to attend to, then best do it now. That's the feeling I got at the time.

'You two are rather quiet?' I ask Mist and Anastassia.

'You will reveal what you know as you make sense of it yourself,' Mist informs me. 'But I believe the event to which Jackson refers is known in my culture as Ragnarök.'

29

Which, to keep it short, entails a battle, many casualties and pretty much the end of life as we know it. More or less.

Mist has become very laid back in her attitude to life since her involvement with Anastassia, to the point that she appears to be under sedation much of the time. It's amazing what love can inspire in some people. A complete, and I hasten to add, positive change in her personality. And for someone who would once have revered Lizzie Borden as someone to aspire to, well, it's taken a bit of getting used to.

Lizzy Borden was accused of killing her father and stepmother back in 1892 with an axe. Although she was acquitted, she nevertheless remained the prime suspect in the case.

At least Mist keeps firm control of her rage now, at least most of the time. I did witness its re-emergence whilst on tour, but the incident in question and her reaction was entirely justified, in my opinion. Some fool thought he'd try his hand with Anastassia and was working some of his best lines. This occurred during a small after-show gathering when Mist had gone looking for a couple of cold beers — both for herself — Anastassia doesn't drink. Upon her return, the lothario found himself pinned to the wall, suspended two feet off the ground by his throat. Now I'm quite sure Anastassia could've managed this impressive feat, but she does have more self-control than Mist. This was no mean feat though, as this guy was solid and must have weighed close to twice what Mist does. At this juncture, Anastassia fully involved herself, proving she was fully capable of defending herself, and she punched a hole in the brickwork right next to his head with that impressive synthetic arm.

That was funny — the look on his face — served him right. Anyway, back to it, I'm drifting off again. I do that at times. Oh, you've noticed.

'You okay?'

J plants a kiss on my cheek, and I'm grinning like a schoolgirl. I can't help myself; we're so made for each other, which reminds me of that time we made a stop just outside Denver at one of those American diners when we were touring. There was a group of four, how can I put it — tattooed fuck-wits — sorry about the language, but you know the type, live in the gym, the rest of the time they spend getting inked, and there's an epidemic of them in the States at the moment.

We were joking around, and some of us had just ordered when I noticed these idiots leering and making inappropriate comments. I don't know about the others, but J and I were very aware of what was being discussed, and I'm not repeating it here. But I salute the others for not batting an eyelid or twitching a mirrored shade if they were aware. Anyway, this went on the entire time we were seated, and once we were finished, J quickly dragged me on ahead of the others and led me to a bright red pickup in the parking lot. He'd picked the image out of one of those idiot's brains if he indeed had a brain. Let's call it a fleshy scatological pustule.

Scatological refers to everything excremental. Shit for brains, in other words!

Right, so I picked up on what J intended straight away. It was bad, but so good as well. But what the hell, these assholes deserved it. The disbelief on their faces when they returned to the parking lot to discover their pride and joy had been crushed down to the size of a cereal packet was a joy to behold.

There I go again, off on a tangent. Keep focused, Alice.

Next is an examination of the dreams — visions — I'd been experiencing over the weeks, much of the same imagery recurring over and over. The coherence of these 'transmitted' impressions was rather discordant, as if the mind sending the visions was, shall we say, not firing on all cylinders. Or, as Deek would put it, *as barmy as a badger in a two-man tent*. I know; what the hell is that supposed to mean? Maybe he experienced an event involving just such a pairing? But I was loathed to ask — sometimes, you're better off not knowing.

That's the impression I got anyway, not the badger metaphor, the other one. Essentially the mind of Nephthys may not be, after I can only presume centuries of self-isolation, as crisp as it once was.

'Perhaps I can assist you?' Ix offers.

Right, we're getting back on track.

Now I trust Ix implicitly, so without having to say anything, J scoots over to give me room and relinquishes me of my cup while Ix kneels before me in preparation.

'I'm going to place you in a light trance which will allow your subconscious to be more readily accessed.'

'Just remember those breathing techniques I taught you,' Kal adds.

I give her a thumbs up and close my eyes as Ix lightly touches my temples with cool fingers. Her skin is always cool to the touch regardless of the weather. It could be in connection with her affiliation with the dead, as out of all of us, she in herself is living proof of life after death after all.

I slow my breathing as Kal had previously coached me, and I feel my heart rate begin to slow as Ix works her own form of magic, and I sink further down into the chair I'm seated on.

'What do you see?' Ix asks; her voice is clear in my mind but distant sounding.

'Nothing,' I hear myself whisper. 'A void... no, wait, I see flashes of colour. Filaments, like threads of rainbow cotton. They're twining together, knitting into a pattern, like a loom. There are symbols.' I can sense a frown on my brow as I struggle to comprehend the images.

'Relax, it is of no consequence,' Ix soothes.

I respond, and immediately the scenario alters. 'I'm surrounded by sand. I'm standing in a vast desert. Great orange dunes tower above me. I can hear the hum of the wind, feel the heat of the sun. There's a figure standing close by, standing at the top of one of the dunes.'

'What is she doing?'

'Watching… waiting… for me.'

'What is she focused on?'

'I can't see from here. She's turning around, beckoning to me. I'm standing at her side. There's a city in the distance. Ancient but… there is modern architecture amongst the older buildings. There's a storm gathering in the distance, like a dust storm stretching out as far as I can see; it fills the horizon. It's closing on our location and consuming everything in its path. The city is no more; all is reduced to dust. The sun is blotted out, and everything is plunged into darkness. The cloud is almost upon us. I can see now that it is composed of the dead, bones, millions of them. They are coming!'

I sit bolt upright, snapping back to reality in an instant to escape the onrush of tumbling bones that threatened to engulf me. Ix has broken contact with me, and she sits back on her heels; she's concerned. I reach out, and she takes my hand. I feel better at once.

'Who's coming?' J asks, moving closer and placing an arm over my shoulders.

'Ragnarök.' Mist repeats her earlier pronouncement.

'I don't know, perhaps.' I slump back, defeated and frustrated.

34

After a few moments of silence, Sophia inserts her thoughts on the subject. 'The Nephilim.' She almost whispers the name under her breath.

She's got everybody's attention.

'It can be the only valid inference. I am... evoking events from an age long since ruined. A time when the Nephilim visited this world, as they have visited many others and tampered with the life forms inhabiting these worlds.'

She's struggling to recall the events, the memories she's sharing with us, vocalised in a maundering way.

Maundering means to talk in a rambling manner or dreamily, which is quite evident to me as Sophia appears distracted and not fully present.

The others are similarly afflicted.

'I, too, am remembering,' Nikki adds. 'The Nephilim were perceived as gods amongst humankind. Creators and manipulators of life.'

'Geneticists,' Kal concludes.

'You mean they are our creators?' Anastassia asks, astounded.

'It would be more accurate to say that they intervened at an early stage in your ancestor's development,' Kal clarifies.

Perhaps it's Kal's spiritual side that's allowing her these insights, but I'm feeling a strong resonance with her words.

'I, too, feel a ninth presence amongst us, one that has always been there,' Mist admits.

And I know what she means. Despite being separated from Nephthys for centuries, I simultaneously feel that she has been with me every step of the way, like a shadow. But magic in itself is hard to explain and quantify. It is merely an as yet unknown aspect of life, something that was introduced to this world by the Nephilim, by all accounts. Of that, I am quite certain now.

'Then is she Nephilim?' J asks.

I can't answer him because I simply don't know.

'A creation of their own that wove itself into life here on Earth, to test its effectiveness. Perhaps even the Nephilim's magnum opus, so to speak.' Sophia is still struggling to voice what I suspect she knows deep within her soul.

'So, she was what? Before she became Nephthys?' Anastassia asks.

'A sentient programme?' J suggests. 'One which became self-aware and created for itself a physical form?'

Sounds plausible to me if we're talking space robots from another dimension.

'And if we interpret Alice's visions correctly, we have to assume that these Nephilim will shortly return for their—'

'Child.' Sophia concludes Ix's sentence. 'She is a child of the Nephilim.'

'Which would explain their previous visitation,' Maddie says. 'Not only in an attempt to locate her but also to test those who would oppose them.'

'An advance guard,' Mist agrees.

'And we intend to oppose them?' Anastassia asks, referring back to Maddie's comment.

'We have to prepare ourselves for that possibility,' Mist informs her.

'She's one of us.' I voice my own opinion. 'We can't stand back and let them carry her off. She's called out to us for help.'

'The consequences of our yielding to their demand may well have dire consequences for us all,' Ix informs us.

'The dust cloud I saw?'

She nods.

'But why now, after so many centuries?'

'Time is relative, Anastassia, particularly to beings like the Nephilim,' Kal ponders. 'Perhaps their experiment has reached its conclusion?' She looks up from where she has been staring at the wooden floor in deep concentration as if extracting ancient knowledge from the very whirls and grains of wood she is sitting upon. 'All things come to an end eventually.'

'I'm with Ix on this.' J speaks up. 'The implications of letting these beings just tear away something — someone — who has been an integral part of life on this planet for goddess knows how long…'

I've got him trained.

'Well, it could be the equivalent of ripping out somebody's heart.'

Nice image there, but yes, he could well be right. I keep visualising that cloud comprised entirely of bones. Another aspect that deeply concerns me also, particularly as I'm the only one present here that's conversant in the practical use of magic, is that the loss of Nephthys could spark significant changes for me personally and prompt serious repercussions throughout the world. Having practised for decades now over many lifetimes, I'm very aware of the intrinsic nature of magic. It suffuses all things, good or bad, woven into the very fabric of things that many of us take for granted, to the extent that few of us are even cognisant of its existence and receptive to its power.

What I'm trying to convey is that if all forms of magic were to be suddenly extracted, then I'm quite sure you'd see and feel the difference all around you. In the gentle caress of a breeze, a poetic diction, a laugh, a loving embrace. Life would become monochrome, not literally black-and-white, but you catch my drift. But then again, I cast my thoughts back to those peacock-coloured filaments drifting through that endless void, and it makes me wonder. What would really happen? Is magic what truly colours life? Nature would therefore become dulled. Laurel and Hardy would still look the same though, but would we still find their antics hilarious?

Hang on, everybody's staring at me.

'Care to share?' Maddie enquires.

'What is your perception of magic?' I ask.

Nikki shrugs. 'An ethereal substratum of reality that exists in much the same way as thought does.'

Hmm, I wasn't expecting that. 'Then what are your thoughts regarding Nephthys?'

'Nephthys can only be a physical manifestation of her corporal self, one which she conceived of to walk amongst us.'

Sounds feasible. 'Maddie?' I'm as well pulling in all their opinions.

'I tend to agree. A being endowed with such abilities would also be deeply ingrained within creation itself but also self-aware enough to want to experience life for herself. To walk the Earth.'

Okay. 'Sophia?'

She's taken to hovering just above her seat, still cross-legged, her light wings shimmering, her aura glowing warmly, a thing she does when she's distracted or daydreaming. And she looks strangely endearing, dressed in her Hello Kitty pyjamas.

'The Nephilim seeded life on numerous worlds and obtruded in the development of many more. Nephthys, as we know her now, was a living essence that wove itself into the fabric of life and altered the course of evolution. I believe even the Nephilim did not foresee that their creation would evolve into such a powerful being.'

Very profound and enlightening; now we're getting somewhere. 'J, any thoughts?'

He's generally the quiet one amongst us, together with Ix. Probably because he's so relaxed and at ease in our company after spending decades trying to block intrusive psychic emanations that pollute the psychic aether. Either that or he feels a bit intimidated surrounded by all us women. I have noticed that he and Deek have become close friends over the months.

'Everything being said is all ringing true with me. I'm getting goosebumps just listening to you all. As you're all aware, I function at a more telekinetic level, and the human brain is still largely dormant, just brimming with untapped potential. And since being with you all, I'm discovering facets of my talents I didn't know even existed. This is big, momentous. I feel all of us, and I mean the whole human race, is teetering on the brink of something pivotal in their development.'

I'm nodding; that's exactly the kind of vibe I'm getting too. But this still could go either way — good or bad.

'Mist? Anastassia?'

'All this magic and superpowers are still relatively new to me,' Anastassia confesses. 'But decades ago, experiments were conducted in Mother Russia researching such phenomenon: clairvoyance, telepathy, telekinesis.'

J's nodding. He's no doubt studied this field himself and is aware of the events to which she is referring.

'But,' Anastassia continues, shrugging, 'a forty-year-old man almost bursting a blood vessel as he rolled a pencil across a table top with his mind, what did it prove? It proved that it would have been far more energy-efficient to simply pick the pencil up. But since those early days, I have witnessed monsters and miracles for myself. I have seen a pickup truck crushed to a size that would fit inside a suitcase and travelled vast distances in the blink of an eye.' She takes a moment to focus before continuing. 'If this person requires our help, then we are obliged to offer her any assistance we can.'

I really like Anastassia, she always speaks her truths, and I'm in total agreement. Also, I could listen to her for hours. It's like tuning in to *Jackanory* — remember that? — but with a Russian accent.

'Or we will die trying,' Mist adds.

I wasn't planning on dying trying but, still, spoken like a true warrior. 'Kal, anything to add?'

'Eastern philosophy is centred around the belief of oneness. The essential balancing of mind, body and spirit. If we allow the final member of our ennead, the keepers of light, to be extracted from our world, then the repercussions can only be catastrophic.'

'The keepers of light?'

'Formed for a specific task: the guardianship of life.'

'Nephthys formed this ennead to protect herself and essentially guarantee the continuance of life on Earth… and beyond,' Mist ponders. 'Warriors of light.'

Now that's a thought. I hadn't considered how this could all affect the afterlife as well. That's Ix's department, and I turn to her next for further details and insight.

'Life is woven together from spirit essence. I have witnessed the unravelling of life many times in the presence of death. Creation is a loom, and Nephthys is the Weaver.'

'This does not bode well for us, then.'

You can say that again, Anastassia. Maria by herself was bad enough, but a whole army of them?

'An army of Nephilim is something we cannot prepare for,' Anastassia continues. 'It reminds me of that time in Dubrovka—'

Her tales from the Motherland never cease to astound me. For someone only in her mid-thirties, she's certainly packed a lot in.

'—when myself and six other *Spetsnaz*—'

Sorry to keep interrupting, but that means Russian Special Operations Forces.

'—were ambushed by a guerrilla faction. We were outnumbered three to one and heavily outgunned. It was apparent that the black market supplied better ordnance than did the Russian army.'

'What did you do?' J asks. He's on the edge of his seat; he loves this stuff just as much as I do.

'We did the only thing we could under the circumstances — we ran.'

Huh! That wasn't quite the ending I was hoping for. 'But you survived to tell the tale. That's something positive, right?'

'I did, yes.'

She looks me right in the eye, her penetrating deep-brown eyes sending shivers up my spine. It's a knack she's got, like Mist's icy-blue stare. I've often wondered what they must feel when they stare into each other's eyes. It must be somewhere between electrifying and terrifying.

'The rest of my crew were less fortunate,' she concludes.

Well, there you have it, to summarise: the Nephilim left something, which has now involved into someone, and now they want it back. And if we just hand her over, it could mean living in a world where everything tastes of tofu and the most exciting programmes to watch on television are party political broadcasts. There may be some of you out there who would see this as paradise. In which case, what are you doing reading this?

Everybody's fallen silent now. I mean, how do you tackle a situation like this? Any ideas? If you can formulate a solution, then post it on the Pariahs website, we'll seriously consider it.

The phone suddenly cuts through the hush, and I think I leap into the air. It never rings, well, hardly ever. I forget I've even got a landline installed most of the time. The last time it raised its shrill voice was months ago now — a cold caller. Nikki answered it before me — they were selling life insurance... or trying to. That must have been the hardest sell of their life, trying to sell life insurance to someone as near immortal as you're likely to find. I just thank the goddess that we're so isolated out here that we don't get Jehovah's Witnesses knocking at the door, as I suspect none would get out alive.

Sophia breezes over before anyone else can react and scoops up the handset, listening intently to the caller for thirty seconds before relaying the details of the call.

'It's Deek. He wants to know if we can get a couple of his mates into Glastonbury?'

Well, that was a crash back down to Earth and reality. Or at least a reality we can readily deal with.

'Sure, what are their names? We'll put them on the guest list.' Glastonbury, hell! I'd forgotten about that after the discussion we've just had.

'Okay, Deek, that's confirmed. Yes, I'll remember. Big Mo and Sal. Okay, see you soon. Bye.'

Big Mo and Sal, I met them when we were in Glasgow. Nice enough couple, but in Deek's own words, 'they're a bit mental'. And funnily enough, Sal is the man in this relationship, five-six and as skinny as a rake, and Big Mo, well, I'm surprised she hasn't crushed her partner at some point over the years, that's all I'm saying.

That's something else to contend with. Not Big Mo and Sal, but preparations for our big gig. Remember I said earlier that I'd slipped some intel we later gathered after the arrival of the Nephilim into the conversation you've just read? Hope you're keeping track? So, with the gig still looming, the Nephilim arriving was essentially just a thought at this stage, a niggling doubt. And there was no way we were going to boycott Glastonbury!

Give me another deranged deity to deal with anytime — that I could cope with.

'We should practise our new song,' Mist suggests.

That is rather trivialising current events, but what else can we do at this stage? The Nephilim hadn't put in an appearance, and until Nephthys makes further contact, we are unable to put a plan of action together.

Our new tune, by the way, is an oldie, well oldish, a cover version. We like to throw one into the mix now and again; it gets the older attendees to our gigs jumping. This time it's 'Looks That Kill.' Guess who unearthed that one in my vinyl collection. Maddie! It's an old Mötley Crüe tune from when I was going through my metal phase back in the eighties.

I wave the band off as they gather themselves. There's nothing further we can do at the moment, and as I'm not an active participant on this track, I plan on taking a walk. I know J will come because he'll need to 'air his head' — as he puts it.

'As long as I'm not intruding, I'd like to accompany you both?' Ix asks.

To be honest, I was hoping she'd tag along, and that about brings you up-to-date, except for those images Maddie 'found' online — almost up-to-date. The only other relevant detail that occurred before the gig was the continued dreams. Although less apocalyptic, I do remember her eyes: the irises a most memorable shade of hazel and rimmed with kohl, a common cosmetic used across Africa and Asia. These staring eyes became a regular part of my dreamscape over the next few days as if they were imparting some unspoken knowledge, but they were in no way intimidating; quite the opposite, I found their presence rather comforting.

While the rest of the band relocated to the practice room, J, Ix and I took to the forest. As it turned out, Ix had something of a revelation herself. There had been an unexpected new development in the realms of the newly departed.

4

'Okay, Ix, what's on your mind?' J gets straight to the point — very little escapes his talented mind.

'There has been an... addition.'

I know instinctually that she's referring to something regarding the in-between place, the place the deceased reside before they continue. But I'm content enough to wait on her to reveal the details of this development when she's ready as I relish the surroundings we currently inhabit. I love this place. It wasn't much of a tough decision when I decided to sell my London home, but I couldn't contemplate giving up this place — it's just so... magical. There, see, that word again, but it's the only word adequate to describe this place. And now I'm seriously considering how I would perceive this wilderness without the presence of Nephthys. Would it just be all right? It's impossible to judge, but it's a possibility I'm very uncomfortable with.

I also notice the transformation this natural haven has wrought on both J and Ix. Ix, in particular, treads these trails imbued with a child-like wonder — skull-face aside.

After we had progressed far enough into the forest so that the faint strains of rock music were no longer discernible, Ix finally speaks of what she hinted at earlier.

'I need to show you both.'

I nod; I'm ready. I've visited this place before, but it will be J's first time, so this will be interesting.

Without further explanation, Ix does what she does and leads us out of this reality into the one the reposing dead contemplate their next stage of existence and transit from one plane to the next — or not, depending on how they had conducted themselves in their previous lives. You know to what I'm referring to — you've made this journey with me before. The trees that punctuate the Canadian forest, blending then fading seamlessly only to be replaced by those sherbet skies, gently swaying grasses and lightly spiced air. I breathe deeply of the fragranced atmosphere and feel all my cares just fade away.

All is much the same as I remember it; meandering spirits and the three gateways, which incidentally J is fully aware of, but now there is the addition of a fourth. This one is situated a little distance away and is round in construction and is obviously what Ix wanted to show us.

J trails us both as he takes in this mystical vista, his agile mind quick to understand the purpose of the three doorways.

'When did this appear?' I ask.

'Recently. As you are aware, time is hard to measure here in this realm, but it is safe to assume that it coincided with your first contact with Nephthys,' Ix explains as we wade through the grass to examine this anomaly in closer detail.

'This is far out,' J exclaims, catching up with us. 'I mean, wow!' He spins around, absorbing the full implications and atmosphere of this place.

'You didn't tell him?' Ix sounds surprised.

'I figured he'd see for himself one day. Besides, how do you accurately describe this?' I make a gesture to encompass the place we currently inhabit. 'It's not so much the place itself as much as the atmosphere.'

J nods; he gets it. 'I understand the purpose of the three doorways,' he says. 'But...' He tails off as we near the round portal.

Beyond the rim, which, unlike the other frames, is solid blue and featureless, it looks as if it's constructed from stone to me, but, in actuality, it could be fashioned from anything. And beyond, there is nothing, just impenetrable darkness. But as we move closer, I can detect movement, slight disturbances within the nihility, like ripples.

'It's like...' I lean closer to inspect the void.

'Your vision?' Ix asks.

I nod; she's right. Flitting within that void are rainbow filaments, barely perceptible to the eye, dancing like microscopic threads of life.

'Magic threads,' I mutter. 'These are the very essence of magic itself, a sort of genetic strand.'

I can tell you that that revelation sent shivers up my spine and across my skull.

'So, this is the source of your powers?' J peers into the void too, mesmerised by the twirling strands.

I take his hand and nod. I'm overwhelmed with emotion.

'But why has it suddenly appeared here, of all places?'

'Watch,' Ix urges.

We stare intently as the coloured filaments —you know what they remind me of? Have you ever watched a nature documentary charting life in the deep oceans? Those creatures that move through the depths by beating hair-like cilia and catch the light when filmed, beating a rhythm of rainbow colours — well, that's a pretty apt description of what I'm witnessing. Then I see what Ix has encouraged us to watch out for as two strands combine, knitting together to form a larger filament.

'It has been happening more frequently and with a more coordinated pattern,' Ix informs us.

'But why?'

'I was hoping that you could shed more light on this matter as you yourself are a purveyor of magic?'

'Sorry… but I'm…' I shake my head. I'm unable to explain this. But, simultaneously, I feel in my gut that I know. If that makes sense to you?

It was how I felt after reading *A Brief History of Time* by Stephen Hawking. I read it intently from cover to cover, but after finishing it, I was none the wiser. It was as if some part of me understood, but, consciously, I perhaps connected with about three per cent of what he was trying to convey. Maybe I'm being a little harsh on myself with only three per cent, but still, much of it was beyond my capacity to grasp.

'It's like staring into the very heart of creation itself.' J conveys his feelings regarding this mystery.

He's right. 'But what is being created?' That's the big question. 'Have you shared this with any of the others?'

'Not yet. But I see no reason why we should withhold this from them now.'

We stand for a while longer, captivated, pointing out further strands as they collide and weave themselves together. This must be what Ix was referring to when she spoke of a loom of creation.

When we finally withdrew, we exited that realm baffled but exhilarated and — sorry to kill the moment — hungry.

That's what I wanted to share with you. The rest of the Pariahs are now fully aware of this development, although nobody could shed any further light on the matter beyond what we had established. We'll just have to be patient and wait and see what develops.

It's time to bring ourselves fully into the present, silent companion, as we head back to New York, where we are still recovering from the exertions of the gig and the arrival of Maria. I say, Maria, it's a force of habit. It isn't actually the same Nephilim, at least I don't think so, as this one was metallic silver in colour. All respect to the band for finishing the set despite the unexpected arrival. Maddie strutted up and down the stage to 'Looks That Kill', chanting the chorus whilst Nikki glared into the crowd, her red eyes flaring in the gloom to appreciative cheers from the crowd. It was the first time either of them had made an appearance on stage, and they were lapping up the attention.

As soon as the final chord faded away and the lights were killed, I located Deek and gathered the team and, casting a portal, whisked us off to New York, the safest of my two remaining residences. And since the Nephilim had returned, it wouldn't be long before the military made an appearance as well. And I had no doubts that they'd be very keen to question us about this worrying advent.

5

It's strange being back here. The last time I visited was when I was retrieving Maddie and Nikki in what seems like years ago now — so much has transpired since then.

Although the apartment is open plan and spacious, it still feels somewhat claustrophobic with us all packed in. Deek still looks rather bemused, a tin of beer in hand. I couldn't very well leave him behind as I have no doubt that the military would have quickly scooped him up after discovering the rest of us had absconded.

The place is more cluttered than I remember it, particularly since the addition of numerous busts, statues and figurines Maddie has displayed on shelves, tables and the floor. I pick up a particularly detailed rendering of a cupped hand that resides on the table nearest the front door and marvel at the design. She has certainly got an eye for detail.

'That one's real, or it used to be,' she comments casually as she notices my interest.

'What?'

'Somewhere to keep the keys to the apartment.' She shrugs.

I tentatively replace the object with open disgust. The same kind of disgust at which I would relinquish my hold on an ossified dog turd, and I throw her a dark look.

'Its previous owner no longer required it, and for once in his miserable existence, he is making himself useful. Part of him at least.'

Just so you know, Deek is now familiar with Nikki's liquid diet and Maddie's part-time involvement in regard to leftovers disposal. And, as with many aspects of life, he took the news in his stride.

Now that we are all settled, the television on so we can keep abreast of events, we quickly come to realise that this incident spans the entire globe.

Whilst we absorb the news coverage, which after a short time begins to become surprisingly boring as none of the Nephilim have moved at all since their arrival, I call out for takeaway — needs must. The others rarely eat, but Kal ordered sticky jasmine rice and steamed vegetables on this occasion. She says drumming works up an appetite. And Sophia indulged with the thinnest slice of J's Margherita pizza.

Nikki went out to dine after I reiterated that the delivery person was not part of the takeaway package.

We were still buzzed from the gig but now also deeply concerned by the return of the Nephilim, and we sat munching in silent contemplation after discussing the situation, many of the details of which I shared with you earlier, whilst Maddie set up the apartment laptop and hacked several supposedly unhackable systems.

Which I'm quite sure would earn us all an all-expenses vacation to Guantanamo Bay if discovered.

'You think they're here to wipe out the human race?' Deek asks in between mouthfuls of some awful looking meat kebab thing. 'Like *War of the Worlds*?'

Now there's a thought. I don't know what to say to that; it's not something I've seriously considered. 'Then we're screwed,' I finally answer. 'Maria by herself was challenging enough, but this…'

'You think?' Mist pipes up. 'She fell before my might with ease.'

'I too—'

I hold my hand up, cutting off Maddie before she can boast of her prowess. 'Okay, not so much a challenge then. But an army of them?' That shut them up. Deek's been briefed, by the way, after we picked him up in Glasgow, so he knows the score, or as much of it as we could relate within the time we had in hand and what has so far been discussed.

'That's what I figured,' Deek answers, completely unfazed.

You'd think he was watching the actual movie and not minute-by-minute real-life coverage.

'Unless the military nukes the shit out of them first,' he concludes.

That's an even more worrying thought. Unlikely as it sounds, it could very well be a serious future threat to take into consideration. I've suddenly lost my appetite.

'You should view this.' Maddie captures our attention and, with a few simple commands, projects the images displayed on the laptop onto the television screen. The grainy but unmistakable image of a Nephilim appears before us, now facing off against what appears to be a mobile missile launcher.

'Where's this?' J asks.

'North Korea.'

'How the hell… you know what I don't want to know.' And I don't… not really.

We watch on in silence, and nothing happens for a few minutes. Neither side is making a move, the Nephilim completely stoic in its attentive stance. Then without warning, a missile is launched. The Nephilim still doesn't respond and literally absorbs the projectile. I mean, it appears as if she took a direct hit, but the missile is just 'swallowed'.

You may have noticed that I keep referring to these Nephilim as female. Well, as I'm sure you'll have noted, any we have seen for ourselves are all very similar in design to Maria. Their metallic exoskeletons, at least, fashioned to resemble female humanoids. Perhaps they are all one gender? Who knows? Maybe it's only us that make a distinction between male and female. Or maybe they chose this form to incite trust. Well, they failed on that score.

Seconds later, the missile returns, streaking out of the Nephilim's torso and wiping out the launcher and deployment of troops in attendance in a ball of smoke and fire. As the dust settles, we can all plainly see the Nephilim is unscathed and still dormant.

'Well, they'll no be needin' their breakfasts the morn,' Deek comments, referring to the now obliterated soldiers.

'Hah!' Maddie barks a laugh.

The plight of mortals to her, particularly incidents such as the one we've just witnessed, is something she finds highly amusing.

'What else you got, Mads?' Deek enquires, downing the remaining contents of his can and setting it aside.

'This piece of footage is from Somalia.'

The scene instantly changes to one of a shanty town, the air thick with dust as a mob of at least a hundred people crowd this particular Nephilim. Many are armed with rifles, and I'm sure I can spot several grenade launchers being hefted as well. This time the people aren't even allowed the opportunity to launch an attack. Perhaps these beings are telepathically linked, and this one is now aware of the recent assault in North Korea.

She lifts one arm, the palm face down, and sweeps it over the heads of those gathered before her. I don't see any light beams being emitted or anything else for that matter, but the result is staggering as everyone present, including those stationed at her rear, collapse like toppled dominoes. She then casually lowers her arm and resumes her static vigil. I do not doubt that these people will never rise again.

Another image is quickly posted from somewhere in the Urals, I think, which shows a jet fighter targeting one of the Nephilim. Its full payload of missiles has no effect whatsoever. And with a barely imperceptible inclination of the giant's head, the jet explodes.

Next, a tank, judging by the insignia stencilled on its side, Chinese in origin, is similarly obliterated before it can even position itself and launch an attack. The twisted remains are barely recognisable in the aftermath.

'I've seen enough.' Talk about dulling the shine of the awesome gig we just staged. I'd been looking forward to that event for ages, and now it's as if it never happened.

'Are they here for this Ne—'

'Nephthys,' I finish for Deek. 'We believe so.'

'Holy shit!'

I've missed his Scottish candidness.

'There is nothing holy about these beings,' Sophia informs him.

'Well, aye, I ken that. What I mean is *holy shit*!'

Sophia still struggles at times with his use of language and turn of phrase.

'So, are ye gonna hawnd this…'

'Nephthys.' I sigh.

'Aye her, over to these Nephilim?'

'That action would spell dire consequences for the human race,' Ix informs him.

'Dire as in the end of the world dire? Or...' He tails off as he considers a comparison he can get his head around. 'Like I smashed ma motor, and it's completely totalled? Or it's not that bad, Tam'll be able to fix it up nae bother?'

'I'm going to go with totalled,' J answers, trying to conceal his smile at Deek's analogy.

'Oh right,' he says before repeating his earlier observation. 'Holy shit!'

'The Pentagon has just announced that DEFCON 2 is in effect,' Maddie informs us all from where she is still engrossed with the laptop.

'Have they just publicly announced this?' Things are quickly heating up, and I'm quite sure that we'll see DEFCON 1 in a matter of hours.

'No, not publicly,' she admits. 'I'm in their secure system.'

'Will you shut that thing off? Before we have a SWAT team abseiling down the front of the building.'

'Very well.' She complies in reaction to my mounting temper and closes the lid. 'But you have nothing to concern yourself with. I bounced the signal through several servers in Europe and Japan before routing the signal here.'

'When did you learn to do that?' Deek asks, impressed by her newly acquired skills.

'It is a simple enough procedure. I will educate you in its operation if you wish?'

'No, you will not.' Secretly I'm impressed too.

Deek throws up his hands in defeat. 'No, you're all right, Mads. I can barely manage to order a pair of baffies off Amazon.'

'What are baffies?' Sophia asks, confused.

'Baffies? Slippers, ya ken, for ya feet.'

She nods in understanding, but I can still read the confusion in her eyes.

'Could you find out about Area 51 on that?' Deek encourages.

'No, she can't.' I'm eager to steer the conversation away from matters that could result in irate people hammering at the door clutching warrants.

'I wouldn't mind knowing about that myself,' J adds with a sideways glance at me.

The look I conjure curtails further discussions on the subject.

'We need to formulate a strategy,' Kal concludes as she chews thoughtfully on a shitake mushroom. 'We need to strengthen our contact with Nephthys as she may have a solution as to how best to deal with these Nephilim.'

'Maybe, but how? Alice is the only one who has a direct line, and only via protracted dream states.'

J's right. And recently, I'm having to re-evaluate my own perception of the magic I tap into. The truth now is that it is generated by a living being, one probably engineered by the Nephilim themselves. So, all in all, I'm stumped as to how best to continue.

'Could we no perform a séance or summat?'

'She's not dead, Deek.' But you know what? He may be thinking in the right arena.

'I may have a solution.'

All heads turn as one and lock onto Ix.

'Magical abilities can be enhanced by the consumption of certain psychotropic plants. Indigenous tribes have been utilising their properties within shamanic ritual ceremonies for centuries to commune with the spirits that inhabit other realms.'

'You talkin' about mushies?'

'What are mushies?' Sophia asks.

'He means hallucinogenic mushrooms,' I translate.

'Aye, that's what I said.'

Unperturbed, Ix continues. 'There are many spirit plants, each with their own particular properties and uses. I believe that there is one that may fit our specific requirements.'

'You want us to take a trip?' I'm less than enthusiastic.

'Well, I'm out.' Deek leans back, signalling his intent. 'Last time I indulged, I spent six hours barricaded in ma mate's shed.'

'Why?' Maddie asks.

'Cos the goblins were after me,' he explains, a little embarrassed.

'Goblins do not exist,' Kal informs him matter-of-factly.

'Do they, no?'

'No.'

'Well, if I'd a kent that then.'

'But there are far worse creatures that do.'

'Yeah, like what?'

'You do not wish to know.'

Deek ponders on this for a moment before accepting Kal's word for it.

'The ritual will only require eight of us. The ennead,' Ix reveals to Deek's obvious relief.

No chance of me bailing then on the basis that the pixies might get me.

This statement finally goads Mist into action, who, up until now, has been quietly cuddled up with Anastassia on the couch. Her taut reaction as she sits forward and her intense look are obviously in response to the thought of excluding her wife from the forthcoming trip.

'I will be fine.' Anastassia places a soothing hand on Mist's knee. 'Deek and I will guard over you all while you journey.'

'When do you intend to perform this ritual?' Mist decides she might as well involve herself now.

'As soon as I can locate the correct species of plant,' Ix informs her. 'I see no reason to delay further.'

'I ken a few dodgy characters who could maybe help ye out,' Deek offers before turning to Mist. 'And you've been awfy quiet.'

'I find the rigours of performing on stage very therapeutic. It relaxes me,' she explains.

'You smashed up two guitars!'

But not her beloved axe-shaped one, I hasten to add. She buys cheap electrics online for the sole purpose of trashing them on stage.

'Exactly,' she informs Deek.

That's the Mist I know of old.

'Thank you for the offer, Deek, but this plant, in actuality the bark of a tree, is particularly rare and can only be found in remote parts of the highland jungles of Peru.'

'Och ye dinnae ken ma sources.'

Ignoring Deek, J steps in. 'I'm not aware of this bark; it's not something I've heard of.'

'Not many have,' says Ix.

J has admittedly dabbled with certain hallucinogens over the years in his younger days, and he is openly quite excited about the prospect. We've shared a lot in our time together — not drugs, I hasten to add — and now it feels like I've known him forever, and in a way, I have. I can certainly connect with Mist's compatibility with Anastassia — the changes I've seen in her are very profound in a very positive way. I can't even recall the last time I saw her wielding her axe, except, of course, her electric one.

'Well, I've never come across it during my studies,' he admits.

'You studied ethnobotany?' Kal enquires.

'In a sense, yes.'

'He indulged.' I elbow him playfully in the ribs.

'The best form of study is in active participation.'

'I, too, have experienced the effects of such plants,' Anastassia admits in a tone of voice that announces the commencement of one of her tales.

Is there anything she hasn't experienced?

We all wait in silence, encouraging her to continue.

'It was an experiment in covert warfare. To see if the ingestion of certain substances could enhance a soldier's effectiveness in the field.'

'Norse warriors were also known to consume *amanita muscaria* before commencing battle, entering a berserker rage,' Mist informs us. 'Was the experiment successful?'

'Partially,' she admits. 'It was the very same substance that the Norse warriors ingested. The fly agaric.'

I'm on the edge of my seat, waiting on the outcome.

'Two of my comrades beat each other to death with their bare hands. A third stripped naked and ran off into the forest. The fourth kept quoting lines from Dostoevsky until I knocked him out with one punch. I don't like Dostoevsky; I find his work depressing. I myself laughed a great deal… then I cried a great deal. The dawning sun, I remember, was quite breathtaking though, but overall, the experiment was an unmitigated disaster.'

'What happened to the guy that ran off?' Deek asks before I can ask the very same thing.

'He was never found,' she answers ominously. 'He may still be living out there in the wilds somewhere.'

'Och, you're windin' me up.'

'Yes, he is most assuredly dead. If the wolves didn't hunt him down, then the bears would have sealed his fate and devoured him.'

Well, on that cheery note, I can't say I'm any more enthused about the journey ahead of us. But right now, I haven't any better suggestions.

'We are in agreement then?' Ix asks us.

Nobody disagrees, is all I can say, but neither is anyone particularly excited about it. Maybe J is a little; maybe some of his enthusiasm will rub off on me.

Nikki makes an entrance at this point in proceedings, solidifying in the living room after shadow phasing through the front door, as she does, even if it's not locked. 'Doors are designed for mortals,' she would proclaim when questioned. Well, I suppose she has a point.

'What have I missed?'

Her eyes are glowing like smouldering embers, and she emanates power, like radiating heat, exuding life force. A consequence of her recent partaking of the red stuff.

'Feeling better?' Deek asks as she takes a seat.

'One less drug dealer the local police force has to contend with.' She smiles wickedly.

'Ix is going to lead us on a spirit journey in an attempt to make contact with Nephthys.' I update her, keen to steer the conversation away from the subject of exsanguination.

She nods as she contemplates the news. 'Once we have made contact, the Nephilim will undoubtedly make their move.'

'You think?'

'Undoubtedly, Deek. If they had access to her now, they would have done so already.'

That had also just occurred to me too.

'We have to trust that when our ennead is complete that a solution to this imbroglio will become apparent.' She rolls the word 'imbroglio' around her mouth when speaking, enjoying the sound of the word on her tongue.

Imbroglio — an extremely confusing and complicated situation. You can say that again!

'We will not yield to these Nephilim. If it is required of us, we will take as many with us into the afterlife as we are able.'

Okay, Mist, I appreciate the commitment, but these 'geneticists' have quite probably adapted themselves since Maria's visit, and therefore our powers will probably have little or no effect on them. So, their plan being: because of Nephthys' current dispersed state, the Nephilim can't just collect her and are awaiting our intervention. Once, if, we successfully retrieve her, the

Nephilim will then step in and claim their prize and crush all resistance. I think that about sums it up.

'I should begin,' Ix declares, standing up.

'Do you need me to cast a portal?'

'That will not be necessary.' She makes to exit the living room but slowly fades out of this reality before she reaches the front door, a ghostly message lingering in the air before she vanishes completely. 'I will reconvene with you all in Canada. The environment there will be far more conducive for a favourable journey.'

Then she was gone, as if someone had erased her from reality.

'What now?'

What indeed, Deek. Several hours have passed now since the Nephilim landed, or materialised, or whatever it is they do. And right now, a walk in the forest to clear my head could be just what's needed in preparation for what's to come.

'Let's get out of here.'

'Canada?' Kal asks, glancing over at me.

I nod. I can tell she's as keen as me to get back home, where we'll feel safer and, in a sense, fortified, better able to psychologically prepare ourselves.

Everyone readies themselves to leave but not before the remains of our takeaway are bagged up, ready for the garbage chute. I also slip that stone hand in there as well when nobody's looking and double knot the bag.

Then the lights are turned off, and the television is plunged into darkness as I flick the socket switch off.

We're good to go.

I rustle up a portal and breathe deeply of that unmistakable loamy scent exuded by the forest and the refreshing tang of pine scenting the air.

The next thing I remember is being helped up by Kal, spitting dirt!

6

I'm rather dazed and shaky, and Kal hangs onto me as I attempt to regain control of my legs while a concerned and wild-looking J picks pine needles out of my hair. Still somewhat disorientated, I attempt to pat down his spiky-looking hair, feeling like I've just slammed half a dozen tequilas in a row. J's eyes are wired too, the pupils dilated, big and dark.

'What the hell happened?' I finally manage to utter; my tongue still feels a bit like it belongs to someone else. 'And why is your hair all sticking up?'

'Oh, yeah.' He pats at it erratically. 'Fifty thousand volts will do that.'

'What?' I'm still not getting this.

'You were tasered,' Kal explains. 'You, Jackson and Anastassia. The only three that succumbed at least.'

'Is that why I've got dirt in my mouth?' I ask, trying to spit out the residue, not very successfully, as my tongue is tingling as a result of my tasering.

'Probably.'

'How long was I out?'

'A couple of minutes,' Kal informs me.

'You too?' I ask J.

'No, all that electricity boosted my circuits, so to speak, like getting a shot of adrenaline. It created a massive feedback loop, and *bang*!' He points into the forest.

I stare for a bit, not sure what I'm looking for, and then I spot a body lying prone in the dirt, and it's not one of ours.

'Military, special forces, I think,' J explains.

'And the rest,' Kal adds.

'What do you mean? Where's everyone else?'

'Picking them up. Your husband took out the whole lot of them, felled them like trees as soon as he was tasered.'

I look at J, who reminds me of some mad scientist with his mussed-up hair and dilated eyes.

He nods a little too enthusiastically, must still be some of that power surging through his system. 'Whole lot of them, how many do you think, Kal?'

'Couple of dozen at least. Here come the others now. You manage on your own?'

I nod as I test my legs, and Kal moves off to help the others collect the bodies.

'Are they dead?' I'm almost scared to ask as Maddie enters the clearing we arrived in, dragging two black-clad masked soldiers by the legs.

'No, they live.'

'Should I finish them now?' asks Mist as she joins us, dumping the two she has slung over each shoulder.

'No, nobody's finishing anyone off. But everyone's good?' I can't believe our luck considering a crack special unit had been lying in wait for us. We got off very lucky.

'My arm is a little twitchy,' Anastassia comments as she clenches and unclenches her prosthetic, testing its integrity. 'But it appears to be functioning properly.' She dumps the unconscious soldier she's carrying, adding him to the growing pile. 'You were the only one who hit the dirt.'

Great, how embarrassing, even the bionic women remained upright. I suddenly remember Deek — surely, he must have face-planted too? I feel a bit better thinking about this.

'Deek?'

'He's fine. The soldier missed his mark, so he didn't take a hit,' Maddie lets me know. 'He's gone to retrieve the rifle he has stashed here.'

Bloody typical, not even Deek. Maybe I'll rub some pine needles and mud in his hair and make myself feel better. Then again, Deek shears his hair almost down to the wood — what would be the point? I refocus my attention. That's some pile of sleepy soldiers stacking up.

'How many more?' I ask Kal as she drops another six onto the pile. 'Should have them all gathered up with one more trip.'

'Way to go, babe.' I'm mightily impressed with J; this is a lot of people to knock out with just one psychic blast. 'How do you feel?'

'Like I've downed a dozen espressos.'

He doesn't drink them, but I catch his drift.

'You think they have reinforcements at hand?' I'm beginning to regain my faculties now, and I'm thinking about more practical issues.

His wide grin loses a bit of its lustre as he nods. 'Yeah, picked that up loud and clear, just before lights out.' He nods at the pile of special ops. 'There's a large deployment set up in the local town.'

'That was quick,' I admit.

'Probably had them dug in close by since our encounter with Maria.'

He's right; it can be the only explanation. We're just too remote out here.

'Back on two feet, I see,' Deek comments as he reappears, automatic in hand.

'Nice of you to stick around and make sure I was okay,' I jibe.

'Och, you were fine. Fifty thousand volts never hurt anybody.'

I beg to differ, Deek.

Kal returns with the final load, closely followed by Sophia, who has scouted the area for any J may have missed.

'You got them all, J.' She beams. 'What are we going to do with them?'

'A bonfire?' Maddie suggests.

My look says it all.

'Then we drop them in the lake,' suggests Nikki.

'Practical suggestions that don't involve killing them, please.'

'We break their arms and legs, then. They will no longer be a threat to us.'

Mist nods enthusiastically at Anastassia's idea. It's hard to tell if some of Mist's way of thinking has rubbed off on Anastassia or if she was always like that. Talk about a match made in Heaven!

'Which one's in charge?' I give up. I'm not going to get a practical idea out of this lot.

J steps up and lifts their arms and legs until he spots an insignia designating high rank. 'This one, I think.'

Nikki then grabs hold of his arm and hauls him out and dumps him at my feet. The all-black uniform and face-covering give him a very sinister look.

'Why? Do you intend on questioning him?' Maddie asks.

'No, it's because I want to do this. It's just a shame he won't feel it until he regains consciousness.' And with that, I deliver him a kick that I'm sure bruises my toes. 'That's for tasering me.' I feel better now.

'Hah!'

Maddie appreciated it anyway.

'If I had delivered him such a kick, those pathetic orbs of his would have replaced his eyeballs,' she adds.

I catch Deek wincing at this; it's quite a thought.

We can't stay here now, that's for sure. I just pray to the goddess (as far as I'm aware, there is no goddess to pray to any longer, the last one was mad anyway, but it's a force of habit) that Ix returns before reinforcements show up.

'Did ye ken you've got a Nephilim paddlin' in the lake, by the way?' Deek suddenly remembers.

'No, I didn't.' Great!

'What is it doing?' Sophia enquires. She's in full Seraph mode, the hilt of her sword protruding above one shoulder, her golden light bathing us all in its wholesomeness.

'Just stawndin' there.' He shrugs.

'These muppets aren't going to come round anytime soon, are they?' I ask J.

'About an hour, no sooner than that. I hit them pretty hard.'

I kiss him — he deserved that — then I lead the group down to the lakeside.

This Nephilim is a spectacular metallic blue, the kind of shade that would look amazing on a sports car. And she isn't, as Deek put it, 'paddlin', frolicking around in the shallows clutching a plastic bucket collecting pebbles. But standing to attention up to her knees in the cool water.

'We could try frying her?' Deek proposes.

Not a bad idea, and I do consider it for a moment until I recall the images Maddie revealed to us earlier.

'We should try communicating with her.'

Sophia's right, it's the only option we have, and this is the perfect opportunity.

'Feel free,' I offer my friends. 'I'm not wading in there, and I'm still feeling a bit shaky anyway.' Which is true.

Sophia expands her light wings and glides forward as the rest of us fan out, just in case. Although what exactly we would do if Sophia's gesture triggered an offensive response, is another matter.

The Nephilim, though, doesn't respond, and Sophia floats directly in front of its metallic head before asking it what it wants, and to everybody's surprise, it responds.

Her voice is deep and resonant and carries an underlying tone that I can't perceive as anything other than threatening. She reminds me of Darth Vader — if he had been a woman.

'Return that which is ours.'

'There is nothing here which you can lay claim to,' Sophia informs her. Her voice is imbued with a potency I have heard her utilise before whilst maintaining the most incredible vocal range when performing on stage.

'The Weaver,' the Nephilim boomed. 'Return her to us.'

'Who is the Weaver?'

No response.

'Why do you require the Weaver?'

Still no answer.

Sophia repeats the question, but it appears as if the conversation has ended. But as we know who the Weaver is and judging by the force in which the Nephilim have arrived, they don't intend on leaving without her.

Sophia rejoins our ranks and descends with a flutter of golden light as she retracts her wings.

'You pick anything else up?' I ask.

'I sensed another agenda that remained beyond my capacity to discern,' she reveals, lowering her voice. 'They are not here with the sole intent of retrieving the Weaver.'

I'm seeing dust clouds filled with tumbling bones again.

That's exasperating, and we're running out of time. I haven't detected any of my magical tripwires going off yet, but it can only be a matter of time until I do, signalling the imminent arrival of further soldiers, and they're not going to be too happy when they discover the pile we've left them.

'We should prepare,' Mist announces and makes her way back to the house, or more specifically the recording studio, where her axe is stored, and I mean her real axe this time. I know that icy look in her eye from old, and she's been parted from her weapon far too long. I'm not sure how much good it will do on this occasion, but it can't do any harm either.

We all follow in her wake as she leads the way to the studio. It's real state of the art; no expense was spared in its construction. The interior wall not only displays Mist's axe but also Kal's own not inconsiderable collection of swords. The majority of which are of Japanese origin, something she particularly favours, and she frequently checks for further editions to her collection via online auction sites that specialise in militaria.

Upon our arrival, she selects four: two katanas, a tsurugi — a double-edged sword — and a tachi, which is very long and single-edged. I remembered! Kal talked to me at great length about these; she's very knowledgeable when it comes to swords. Together with these, she selects her trusty ebony demon slayer and a vicious-looking curved scimitar. Where she found this last one, I can't recall, probably online as well. It's amazing what you can get delivered through the post these days. No wonder knife crime is rocketing.

The rest of us have to contend with a quick change of clothes once we arrive back at the house as we're still wearing the same gear from the gig, and my top and jeans now have the added addition of mud from when I fell flat on my face.

Once suitably kitted out, we regroup beside Yogi — our stone bear mascot.

Kal has fitted her custom-made scabbard that holds all the tools of her trade, and Mist has her axe holstered and ready for action. Deek has his automatic slung over his shoulder.

The longer we wait for Ix to return, the more anxious I become. The dozing special ops team is worrying me deeply, and this event also marks a new phase regarding our future, and it's not a good one at that. The military will never quit hounding us now, even if we do manage to repel the Nephilim. We've seriously bruised their ego, and that won't be easily rectified.

'Don't worry about them.' J comforts me, drawing me closer with one arm. His hair is almost back to its normal self now. 'I'll sense them if they start to come around.'

I hug him in return and bury my head in the curve of his neck. 'This is so fucked up,' I whisper in his ear.

'Tell me about it, but it was bound to happen sooner or later. The arrival of the Nephilim just sped the process up, that's all.'

He's right. I get that too. It's only our fame and the media coverage that has kept them in abeyance for so long. The problem with most military organisations is that they need to be in control of any situation and the thought of a group of renegades with the ability to render them essentially impotent just wasn't something they were ever going to come to terms with.

I stand up, feeling infinitely better after my hug.

'The Avengers never had shit like this to deal with.' At least I can't recall a situation quite like this one. They were more inclined to fight amongst themselves.

'The X-Men did,' Deek recalls. 'All the time.'

'The Wolverine Jackman would carve up those toy soldiers. The ground would be saturated with their spilt blood.'

Thanks for that, Mist; that's another nice image to contemplate. I'm so thankful now that I never introduced them all to *Deadpool*.

'She is returned.' Sophia lifts off and spins around as she detects the presence of Ix.

Now at least we can get the hell out of here. But where to?

Ix appears out of the shadowy depths of the forest. The sun is setting now, and the light is fading fast. Her skull-face seems to glow ethereally, and she looks like an extra from a George Romero movie — he of the famous zombie flicks. Well, okay, she doesn't quite look like a flesh-eating corpse, but I'm quite sure she might if a group of teens gathered around a campfire were to witness her manifesting nearby in the dead of night, whilst drinking beer, smoking pot and exchanging ghost stories. Do teens even do that any more? Probably not, it's more than likely expensive designer drugs and social media — progress! Anyway, Ix appearing out of the gloom would certainly set them running for the hills, I'm quite sure.

She joins us, clutching a small packet fashioned from a leaf of striking emerald green, fresh from Peru and no doubt containing some of this mysterious bark.

'You have had company,' she states.

'You noticed?' Maddie seems surprised at her power to detect the soldiers who lay hidden further behind the recording studio.

'I sensed their presence as soon as I arrived. And that of the Nephilim.'

'Aye, Sophia had a wee banter wi' it, but it wasn't very chatty.'

'But we can now verify that they are here for Nephthys,' Sophia confirms.

'As we suspected.' Ix nods.

'I also sensed a secondary objective, one which I could not discern.'

Ix meets my eye after Sophia speaks. I know she's thinking the same as me. In all fairness, we probably all are, except Deek, as we didn't have the time to fill him in with all the details. But the rest were there when I shared my dream visions.

'Then perhaps I should attempt to extract further details,' Ix suggests.

'As I said, she's not that talkative,' Deek reaffirms.

'I had a more intrusive method in mind.'

7

We retrace our steps back down to the lake that borders my property. I note that J's fully focused on detecting the tell-tale signs of awakening minds now in case the soldiers heaped together in a pile begin their slow ascent back to consciousness. The rest of the team are also on full alert too. We are fully prepared this time for an attack and not just from the Nephilim, and I feel if that were to occur, then blood would be shed, and that's something I seriously want to avoid if at all possible.

Ix phases into her 'ghost-mode' as we approach. It's the best description I can summon as she flits between the trees like an ethereal mist with the intention of approaching the resident Nephilim from the rear while the rest of us are tasked with distracting her.

Distract her! Perhaps we should sing her a tune? Or reenact a scene from the *Avengers*? We've watched it together often enough. But as we finally gather once more on the shoreline, Deek is already on it, and he's selected a stone and throws it at the blue giantess. It rebounds with a resounding metallic clang off her torso and plops into the water.

That's not exactly what I had envisioned, and I clutch at J's arm and wince as I hear the noise reverberating through the air. I can't help it, and I'm fully expecting her to come to life and deliver us her full retribution.

But nothing happens; she doesn't even stir. I throw Deek a look anyway.

'What? Ix wanted us to keep her occupied.' He defends his action.

'And we will do just that.' Nikki gets onboard now and walks over to my picnic table and lifts the heavy wooden bench with one hand.

Not my bench! But I watch on in silent disbelief as she tosses it effortlessly like a stick at the silent colossus. The solid pine cracks loudly across her face and splits before dropping into the lake with a loud splash.

'I'll fashion you a new one,' Nikki promises as she registers the look of incredulity on my face.

Still no response from the Nephilim.

'I liked that bench,' I mumble.

'Well, it's broken now.' J exerts his power and pulls it back onto dry land.

This time Maddie steps forward. 'It is my turn,' she insists.

Children!

As Maddie picks up the damaged bench, I can see the extent of the damage. Nikki must have thrown it with quite considerable force, and it barely holds together.

As Maddie hurls it, another direct hit, with the same reactionless result, I notice a pale shape gliding across the surface of the water, wraith-like. Deek has also spotted Ix and begins to hail stones at the Nephilim that he has gathered from the immediate area.

In less time than it takes for Deek to throw his third projectile, Ix is upon her, climbing her metallic skin like mist, and she thrusts her hands into the blue helmet.

This finally extracts a reaction, and she reaches up with both arms, intending to remove Ix, but she is too quick and too insubstantial, throwing herself backwards before the Nephilim can make contact. Ix 'ghosts' further, and one massive blue arm passes straight through her ephemeral form.

'Perhaps we should slowly back up,' Kal suggests, holding up all six of her hands to show the Nephilim that she is unarmed.

Anastassia quickly follows suit, dragging Mist back by the arm.

Now that Ix has safely retreated, the Nephilim focuses on the rest of us as we withdraw as a unit, raising her arm in our direction. Sophia hits her with a discharge of divine energy emitted from her unsheathed sword, and the Nephilim takes a step back as she's hit by the full force.

I'm prepared for a full-on attack now, and I put in place a force field, shielding us all as Sophia shuts off her heavenly light. But incredibly, the Nephilim just lowers her arm to her side and becomes inert once again, the shattered remains of my picnic bench bobbing in the disturbed water around her.

'The Nephilim need us intact,' Sophia explains. 'Without us, they can never retrieve their Weaver.'

That makes sense. Nevertheless, we continue our cautious retreat as Ix solidifies and joins us, not turning our backs on the Nephilim until we reach the relative safety of my backyard. I say backyard — it's more of an open area to the rear of the property that Mist cleared of trees during her moody period.

We take shelter in the house, and I notice for the first time that the door has been kicked in, the wood around the lock splintered — I'm not impressed. I would have delivered that soldier a second kick if I'd been aware of that!

Then, suddenly, I feel it. 'Not now,' I groan.

J looks my way, and he knows to what I'm referring straight away.

'Reinforcements,' I inform the others, and a lot of them, judging by the prickling that's running across my scalp as my magical barriers are breached. 'We've not got long, ten minutes,' I estimate.

'Then we need to leave.' Anastassia speaks up.

'Or we can utterly destroy them?' suggests Maddie with a wicked smile, raising an eyebrow above her golden shades.

I know she's just joking. I'm pretty sure she is anyway.

'Did you manage to extract anything useful?' J asks Ix.

She nods, the simple gesture conveying much, and it leaves me feeling hollow inside. But the details can wait for now until we vamoose.

'Anywhere in mind?' J picks up on the thought. 'Vamoose?' he adds.

'Yeah, I like vamoose — we should use it more.' I do have a place in mind, actually, it just came to me in a flash, and I clamber over the couch to reach the bookcase and pull out the heavy atlas stored there.

Maddie sweeps my tea table clear with one arm as I return with the heavy tome. Under normal circumstances, I would admonish her and lecture her lengthily about why we should respect other people's property. I'm also ignoring the spreading pool of melted ice cream that's puddled on the floor and the broken mug — what the hell — this place is going to be overrun by the military soon. I shudder at the thought of all those muddy boots. I place the book on the cleared table and leaf through it until I find what I'm looking for. It was so obvious, really.

'The logical choice.' Kal nods in agreement as she views the map of Egypt laid out before us.

'Are we gonna see the Pyramids?' Deek asks.

'No, the place is probably heaving with tourists anyway.' I wouldn't mind seeing the Pyramids myself.

'Aye, we'd probably get mobbed by them anyway, asking for autographs,' he comments in all seriousness.

Are we a thing in Egypt? I have no idea.

'Here.' Nikki leans over my shoulder and stabs one finger at the map.

I stare at the area she's indicated in the Libyan desert. I can't see any landmarks, and it reminds me of the Empty Quarter we visited in Arabia.

'You sure?' I glance up at her.

She gives me an affirmative nod.

'There's nothing there,' remarks Sophia. 'Just sand,' she complains, folding her arms.

'You have my assurance that there is a site there, but one which you will never locate on any modern map.'

'And you know this how?' I'm curious despite the ticking clock.

'Knowledge of our past returning. Perhaps Nephthys is directing us?'

'There are numerous sacred sites throughout the world that have fallen into obscurity and have been forgotten by modern civilisations,' Ix explains.

'Places shunned and forgotten out of fear,' Nikki concludes.

'Is this place cursed? Like pharaohs' tombs?' Deek asks, concerned.

'Something like that.' Nikki grins toothily.

It all sounds rather ominous, and we're running short on time; our ten minutes must be almost up. At least where we're going should be deserted — as the name suggests. Worst-case scenario is that the Nephilim have posted a guard there, and the military have pitched some tents, and we arrive bang in the middle of camp, and I get tasered again.

'I can hear engines,' Sophia informs us.

'And there's a lot of them,' J adds grimly.

'Okay, grab a hold of each other.'

Everybody clasps hands with the person next to them, forming a chain. As soon as we're all linked in, I feel that energy blossom and I focus hard on the area on the map that Nikki pointed out. I fix the location in my mind's eye and close my eyes, working my magic just as I recognise the distant drone of engines approaching.

The first change I'm aware of is the hard wooden floor underfoot softening and shifting as it's replaced by sand, and, surprisingly, my skin breaks out in goosebumps in reaction to the chill in the air.

I open my eyes. We've arrived, and I was forgetting the time difference. It's a few hours before dawn here, and it's freezing, with nothing surrounding us but miles and miles of endless desert.

8

'There's nothing here,' Deek points out.

'It's a desert,' Nikki responds, shaking her head.

'And it's freezing,' Sophia adds.

You wouldn't think that Seraphim suffer from the cold, would you? But apparently, they do!

'At least it's Nephilim and soldier free.'

'Aye, Alice, I suppose you're right,' Deek concedes.

Sophia takes to the wing with a twirl, with the consummate grace only an angelic being could carry off, pouting, her eyebrows lowered in consternation as she surveys the area. She always reminds me of Tinkerbell when she does that. And despite the inhospitable conditions, deep down, I'm just thankful I'm not staring down the barrel of a gun. But the sheer isolation of this place is oppressive, to say the least.

'Can you feel it?' Nikki enquires as she begins to ascend the dune we arrived on.

'Aye, ma nuts are freezin'.'

I don't think that was what Nikki was referring to, Deek.

'There's something below the sand,' Sophia points out, indicating an area beyond the dune Nikki is scaling.

'Yes, I'm getting it now.' J squeezes my hand tighter. 'It's like a void, like a piece of this place has been removed.'

'Or disguised,' I respond. This has to be the place. Now that I'm aware of it, the absence is unmistakable.

'There are powerful ancient forces still at work here.' Kal senses the anomaly too.

'Nephthys has guided us to this, the last place on Earth she was physically present. She knows we are close at hand.' Ix follows in Nikki's footsteps; the precious package is hugged close to her chest.

And trusting our instincts now, the rest of us begin to climb the dune. It reminds me of walking up a descending escalator, the sand constantly shifting and pulling at our feet, and it takes us several long minutes before we reach the summit where Nikki and Sophia are already waiting for us.

The slight wind is noticeably colder up here, and Deek is rubbing his hands together to generate some warmth as he completes our contingent.

'I didnae think it would be so cold in the desert,' he complains, his breath clouding before him.

'Thought you'd be used to the cold coming from Scotland?' J enquires.

'No, you never get used to it. If I'd kent, though, I'd have grabbed a jacket.'

'Thought you did a couple of tours in Iraq too?'

'Aye, but it was never this cold at night.'

'There.' Nikki points towards a shadow nestled within the hollow between this dune and the next.

On closer inspection, I can make out a distinct hole within the sand, the starlight and clarity of the Milky Way out here shining down in all their beatific glory, casting the area in question into deep shadow. Nikki's instincts and my portal raising placed us exactly where we needed to be. And now, I have no difficulty in believing that our long-lost sister did indeed intervene and guide us here.

'What, the Weaver's doon there?' Deek peers down, squinting, rubbing his arms now vigorously to generate further body heat. 'What she doin' out here?'

'She is not physically present. But this place was her last known location on this physical plane and our best means of establishing contact with her,' Ix patiently explains to him.

After much slipping, sliding and stumbling, mostly by me, culminating in a graceless roll down the last few feet, dragging J by the hand to join me in my tumble, we reach the bottom.

What I could only perceive as a shadow before was now unmistakably recognisable as an entrance leading to an underground system or tomb. The drifting sands had almost buried the entrance completely, and the steps were barely recognisable beneath the heaped sand. I can only assume that Nephthys uncovered this sole entrance for us to find, or perhaps ancient magic set in place, prevented this sacred place from being completely buried over the centuries. Either way, the feeling I was getting was augural.

That's the perfect word to accurately describe the sensation flooding my system — a sign that some good — or bad — event was to shortly transpire in the near future.

My 'spidey' senses were tingling; the magic that permeated this sacred place was old... so old. I admit I was excited at the prospect of continuing and a little spooked. Normally one of the first rules of what not to do — specifically in a horror movie — would be to enter some ancient underground chamber with the prospect of contacting a powerful ethereal being. Particularly if you intend to consume hallucinogens to assist you in your endeavours. This has got all the makings of a supernatural chiller stamped all over it. But first, we'd have to contend with digging the stairs clear as there was no way any of us were squeezing through the gap available.

'You sure this...'

'Nephthys,' I supply Deek.

'Aye, her. You sure she's one of the guid guys? Cos I'm not feelin' too guid aboot headin' doon there.' He's kneeling at the threshold, peering into the depths, the draught cast from below billowing his hoodie gently.

I can fully empathise with what he's feeling. Maybe a doormat with WELCOME printed on it in bright, cheery colours and a nice potted lavender would have certainly improved the overall vibe no end.

'What you are feeling is quite possibly the result of a magical reticulum set in place to mask this place and deter the curious,' Kal informs him and is met with a puzzled look.

'A what?'

I know this one. 'An intricate or fine network.'

'Oh, like a net.'

'Yes.' Doesn't quite have the same impact, though.

'But Deek does make a fair point,' Mist admits. 'Can we be sure that Nephthys is not cast from the same cloth as the Nephilim themselves? They who have proved to be far from hospitable, and that we are merely being played?'

I hope Mist's wrong about that, but I can't be certain. I don't think any of us can be under the circumstances. And that does also raise the question, which I have pondered on before, about Nephthys' psychological stability after all these centuries. I look to J for some sort of reassurance, and as we're still clasping hands, I know he can pick up on my thoughts.

'I'm not picking anything negative up,' he confides. 'Got to admit I am a little nervous, but I've not got a voice at the back of my mind screaming for me to get the hell out of here either.'

'That's guid enough for me,' Deek concludes, standing up and clapping J on the shoulder.

And it's good enough for me too. That reminds me. 'What did you find out, Ix?'

Ix takes a moment to survey us each in turn, her expression sombre, her visage adding a further sinister element to the moment.

Now I'm not feeling so positive. Despite her having the gentlest of natures, she can make my heart skip a beat on occasion, and I've tried to find a fitting description that best fits her appearance. If you have seen images of her, you'll get the gist of what I'm referring to, but each time I think I've got it, then I realise that, in actuality, it's woefully inadequate or misleading. But right now, beneath the starlight, her skin appears translucent, the bone of her skull almost luminous. Perhaps it is just an effect of the light, but I've got to admit that she reminds me of some voodoo priestess — spooky.

'The Nephilim bring ruin to this world; there will be no negotiation, no compassion, just destruction. The annihilation of all. The world will be scoured clean and a wasteland left in their wake.'

Nobody speaks for a moment. Come on, Deek, I'm counting on you now.

'Fuck!'

That will do nicely. I knew you wouldn't let me down.

I'm not one for swearing much. It doesn't offend me, you understand, and it's something most people do from time to time, myself included, when the appropriate situation calls for it. And this was an appropriate situation. My vision was prophetic after all, the end of days — Ragnarök, as Mist would refer to it as. So, here we are again facing extinction, though, in retrospect, I think this situation is far worse.

'Then our only salvation lies with this Weaver they covet so much?' Anastassia speaks up.

'It certainly looks that way,' I answer.

'What if we were to give the Nephilim what they want? What then?'

'Regardless, Deek, they intend to exterminate all life here,' Ix clarifies.

It's a strong feeling I harboured myself, that once, if, the Nephilim retrieved Nephthys, we were then going to be ground into the dirt.

'Have your dreams not elucidated you further?'

'I'm sorry, Mist. I've tried, but beyond what I've shared… it's like the connection is still there, but the volume has been turned right down.'

'I've even attempted to boost the signal,' J adds. 'Tried to psychically enhance the connection or fine-tune it somehow. Sometimes I pick up images when Alice was still asleep, but they flash up so quickly that I can't grasp their meaning.'

I know what he means; we've discussed it before. There's this scene in a movie — I can't recall which one — and there's an image played, a car driving across the screen and disappearing then reappearing at the other side. The process is repeated and sped up until the flashing image of the car disappears from view, but you know it's still there, it's just moving too fast to visually perceive. That's a pretty fitting description, I think.

'Then we must continue as best we can and pray to the goddess that our ennead will rise victorious against these Nephilim.'

Well put, Mist, and what else can we do? The extreme situations we are faced with and the danger all that entails, and still the military kick my door in and taser me! I'm not going to forget that one in a hurry.

'So, what exactly is this place?' Anastassia has now taken up Deek's former position as she peers into the subterranean darkness. 'A tomb?'

'In that it was a final resting place for a physical body, then yes,' Kal explains. 'A body that has long since departed.'

'Tomb robbers?' Deek pipes up.

Nikki just casts him a look, and he shuts up.

'Nephthys achieved goddesshood within her time on Earth. She constructed a physical form to walk this Earth, and when the time came to exit this realm, she created this place, its completion actuating her next phase... her transformation in a sense,' Ix elaborates.

'This is so much more than a tomb,' Kal expands.

Then I get it. 'It's more like an appliance... a machine.'

'Exactly.' Ix smiles as I grasp what she is trying to convey.

Of course, it makes sense now. Nephthys, or whoever she was before she wore that mantle, originated from a culture so far in advance of our own. Their technology light-years ahead of us, even now.

'Wow!' J exclaims. 'My head is buzzing. That's exactly it; why didn't I see this before?'

'We are merely human after all,' I console.

'Deek, this is total sci-fi, mate.' J slaps Deek on the back.

Both J and Deek are big sci-fi geeks, not so much that the two of them would go to conventions dressed up as stormtroopers or something, but they often discuss the intricacies of cult and modern classics, much of the detail is even lost on me, and I'm a big movie buff myself.

'Is it?'

Deek doesn't seem very convinced; all he can see at the moment are some steps.

'To think we probably stood on this very spot, the eight of us, centuries ago. Gathered together for what was possibly the final time until Alice freed us.'

Sophia's words run through me like cold fire. I hadn't even considered that likelihood until I heard her words. And she's right. It's like crossing our own timelines. I wonder who I was back then? Who we all were? It's all becoming so clear to me now.

'Nephthys guided us in the construction of this place. She knew the Nephilim would return for her and so planned her escape, dispersed herself within the fabric of life,' Nikki confirms.

'You lot built this place?' Deek's eyes are wide with surprise.

'We were involved, yes. But not as you see us now; it was our former selves.'

I suppose Deek just sees us as his mates and never really considers our past and who we were and what we really are. But the expression on his face right now is priceless.

'She intended that if she could no longer find herself, then neither could the Nephilim,' says Sophia.

'That — she tasked to us,' I conclude.

'But why hide from her own people? What happened?'

'I'm afraid I can't answer that, Deek. Perhaps she became more endowed with human qualities, became more compassionate. Her eyes opening to the error of her maker's ways. Not everyone's parents know what's best for their offspring.'

'Aye, I hear that, Alice. I'm just concerned that she'll turn out to be like that mad bitch we sorted oot in the underworld.'

'Magic is pure chaos energy. Its wildness can be utilised for good and bad purposes. It's the practitioner that makes that choice, not the source.'

'I get that.' He nods. 'So, as long as she's one of the Pariahs, we're good, but if the Nephilim get their claws into her… it's goodbye happy hour, doon the Chieftain.'

That's pretty much it, Deek!

'One must still have chaos in oneself to give birth to a dancing star,' Kal recites quietly.

'Friedrich Nietzsche,' J identifies, impressed.

J might be a bit of a movie geek, but he's super intelligent too. And what did I tell you about Kal and her reading tastes?

'Then the fate of the world lies in our palms,' Anastassia summarises, standing up from her examination of the steps. 'Then we will not fail.' She holds out a fist, and Deek fist bumps her.

'Hell, yeah,' he agrees wholeheartedly.

Finally, we have pretty much the full picture now. The Nephilim are awaiting us to retrieve Nephthys, then using her power, destroy humanity. Why? I don't know. Maybe they just got bored of us and want something new to play with. And if we fail to comply and walk away, leaving Nephthys in her current state, they will destroy humanity. Talk about a rock and a hard place. This makes me ponder over Sophia's words when she said they had been instrumental in the advancement of other races. How many other planets have played host to their machinations? How many planets have also been wiped clean of all life? Mars — there's a thought — was the red planet once teeming with life? Perhaps as advanced and intelligent as ourselves? The Nephilim then moving on to the next available planet in this solar system — ours — and starting afresh, Mars left barren in their wake. It certainly gets the mind thinking.

'We should clear this entrance.'

Yes, Kal's right. It seems like we've been standing here gabbing for ages... reminiscing... remembering. It's time to get to work.

I have to be completely honest with you here, Kal did the majority of the excavating. Six hands work far more efficiently than two, and there wasn't much room for anybody else to work alongside her. J helped, though, by psychically pushing the excavated sand out of the way so it didn't trickle back down the shaft. And between the two of them, the stairs were soon revealed, black stone weathered smooth by centuries of abrading sand. It still took about an hour for the staircase to be sufficiently cleared to allow us full access, though, and when the way was freed, we descended single file into the depths.

9

'I hope there are no mummies doon here?' Deek calls from the back before adding, 'I'm only kiddin', Alice.'

Still, I could do without that kind of imagery, Deek.

Sophia blooms into life as we are swallowed by the impenetrable darkness wrapping us within her golden divinity.

'Och, you're an angel, Sophia,' Deek says appreciatively.

And so am I. I always feel so ill-prepared for outings like this; the last time I forgot to bring my shades, this time, it's a torch.

'I am no angel, Deek.'

I was waiting on that.

'I am Seraphim.'

'It disnae matter,' he mutters.

I know what he meant, but sometimes it's best to let things ride rather than become entangled in a long-winded discussion. Particularly regarding such subjects as the difference between an angel and a Seraphim.

'We may encounter guardians, though,' Nikki calls back over her shoulder to Deek from where she leads the group with Ix close behind her.

Don't tell him that, Nikki. Or me, for that matter!

'You're windin' me up, right?'

'No.'

'You coulda just said yes to reassure me.'

Fair comment, Deek, she could!

'Then I would have been lying.'

'What form would these guardians take?' asks Maddie, who is directly behind J and me.

'Magical constructs are more Alice's field of expertise.' Nikki passes the buck.

I don't want to talk about this! I swallow, but my mouth is quite dry; it must be the air down here. '*If* any remnants are guarding this place, then they could quite literally take on any form.' And I'm not lying — they could. 'But because essentially Nephthys originates from a world completely alien to our own, the guardians may be far more...' I struggle to find the right words.

'Alien?' Deek asks.

'Yes, like those pods the face-huggers leap out from,' J answers seriously, but I can feel the suppressed laughter wracking his body.

Between Nikki and Maddie, and J and Deek, when they get started, I feel like I'm running a crèche sometimes.

'No, not like face-huggers; he's winding you up. Listen, can we stop talking about guardians and aliens, please?'

'I never mentioned aliens,' Nikki reminds me. 'That one is on you.'

'Well, it wisnae funny, J,' Deek calls out.

'I still owe you for that time when we were on the road.'

'What time?'

'When you mixed tabasco in with the ketchup, remember?'

'Och aye, that was funny.'

'No, it wasn't. I spent hours on the toilet after that.'

'Yes, the facilities were most unsavoury following that event,' Mist recalls. 'Shall I punch him for you, J?'

'Hey, come on,' Deek beseeches. 'It was jist a prank.'

'It's okay, Mist, but thanks for the offer,' J responds. 'Everybody just chill.'

'Bet you could've done with summat chill back on that bus.' Deek sniggers.

'Hah!' Maddie barks.

'We should be vigilant.' Ix lowers the tone of her voice, reminding us of the seriousness of the situation. 'Her mind may be unstable after so many centuries of dispersal.'

'But she kens we're on her side, right?'

'We shall see,' Maddie answers.

'So, she might be nuttier than a peanut farm.'

That's as good an analogy as any, I suppose. But I hope she is aware of our good intentions; I'm convinced she is, in fact, and besides, the last thing I feel ready to confront right now is another deranged deity and her guardian entourage.

10

Steps... so many steps!

The atmosphere is filled with an expectant hush; the only noise is our footfalls on the ancient stone as we descend ever deeper. And now, I can't help but visualise mummies wrapped in decaying bandages lunging out of the depths with grasping skeletal hands.

Thanks for that, Deek!

Even Sophia's angelic phosphorescence does little to dispel my anxiety, but it wasn't just the thought of what might be lying in wait for us below that was troubling me. I feel J give my hand a comforting squeeze.

'One problem at a time, Alice.'

He knows exactly what's preying on my mind, the presence of the military force which has by now taken over our home. You might think that your partner being aware of your innermost thoughts as being intrusive — perhaps if you've got secrets to hide — but that's something we don't have, and in many ways, having someone so in tune with yourself can be very... stimulating, if you know what I mean.

'Can't help it. I loved that place, and now it's just ruined. I'll never feel safe there again.'

'It was bound to happen.'

He attempts to console me, but I know as well that he feels the same; he loved that place just as much as I did. There's no solution to this, we can only relocate, but then it will undoubtedly only be a matter of time before we're tracked down yet again.

'A conflict is inevitable,' Kal surmises from where she is descending the steps in front of me. 'The question is, how are you prepared to deal with the problem?' She glances back over her shoulder as she asks.

That's precisely it. Do we move and keep running? And I'm not willing to rely on our newfound fame to protect us forever from the military, and worse. Or do we make a stand and fight? I know that several members of the team would have no qualms if it came to the latter, and I appreciate the fact that they do look to me for guidance regarding such situations — it means a lot to me. But not only have I got J and myself to consider, but all of us, not least of all Anastassia and Deek, who, together with myself and J, are still very susceptible to bullets.

'We have reached the end of the stairs,' Nikki informs us from the front, and we all come to a standstill.

At last!

'The way is blocked.'

'Blocked how?' I ask her.

'See for yourself.'

I squeeze past Kal, which is easier said than done in the confined space, and then past Ix to join Nikki. Before us lies a solid wall of blank stone. I run my fingers along one side where it meets the wall of the staircase.

'There's no seam here at all,' I remark. 'It's like it was carved from a single piece of stone.'

'Then it will require a magical conjuration to grant us entry into the room beyond,' Nikki concludes, edging back past me to allow me space. 'We are at your dispensation.'

The portal I establish appears within the barricade of stone, creating a round doorway through which we pass.

We've reached our destination, a cavernous hall, the dimensions of which I can roughly gauge by the echo our footsteps produce as it's blindingly dark. Its size now justifying the countless steps we have just navigated to get here.

'Hello!' Deek calls out, his voice echoing into infinity as we tread carefully further into the vault. 'I dinnae think there's anyone home,' he concludes after a few seconds.

'What did you expect? Tea and biscuits?' I'm a bit edgy, my nerves frayed.

'Naw, but a wee dram wid be most welcome.'

Sophia guides us with her light towards the wall to our right, her golden aura, although providing us with some comfort, cast the shadows beyond her light into darker obscurity.

The wall, like the steps and ground beneath our feet, is carved from the same black stone; the entire surface, as far as I can tell, is incised with ancient Egyptian script. I run my hand over the archaic symbols, many of which I don't recognise but still seem familiar to me. But I quickly locate the glyph that represents Nephthys, resembling as it does a bowl resting atop a pedestal.

'These Egyptian hieroglyphs are interspersed with the language of the Nephilim,' Sophia informs us from where she floats several feet above our heads.

Then at least we've arrived in the right place. Although, that was something I never doubted.

'Powerful,' Kal whispers as she too runs hands over the cool stone of the wall. 'You can still feel the magical vibrations after all these centuries.'

I replace my hand at hearing this, and it's true, barely perceivable, but yes, a very faint vibration is detectable as if an electrical charge is running through the walls.

'J?' I always like to get his view on things like this.

'I've never experienced anything like this. I feel like we're standing in the very heart of a power generator. The energy in this place is off the chart.'

Sophia touches down like a feather, slowly succumbing to gravity. 'This channel appears to be filled with oil,' she points out.

I look down and, sure enough, set along the base of the wall is what looks like a shallow gutter. I crouch down and dip my finger in the channel, smearing the substance that it holds between my fingers and taking a tentative smell.

'Anybody got a lighter?' Of course, they don't, so it's up to me. My elemental magic is a little rusty, but with the energy coursing through this place, I'm quite sure I can conjure a little spark. Almost as soon as the image of fire is formed in my mind, the oil ignites, the flame rushing off in either direction as the flammable oil catches alight.

We stand and watch as the flame recedes into the distance, finally revealing to us the true scale of this place.

'This structure is immense,' J comments, awestruck by the sheer scale. 'But it seems familiar somehow.'

'That's because it is,' I confirm.

'I know, but it's still a lot to contend with, visiting our pasts like this... old haunts.'

The hall is still mostly sheathed in darkness, but now we can at least make out the massive columns that support the roof high above like immense tree trunks, their surface also decorated with ancient glyphs. But apart from these additions, there appears to be little else here, no ornamentation, altars or — I'm glad to report — mummified creatures.

As soon as we arrived, Nikki had drifted off into the darkness to reconnoitre the area quite at home within the tenebrosity. That word beautifully sums up this place and Nikki's personality as well.

I first spot her coal-red eyes floating in the gloom before the rest of her materialises, and she drifts up behind Deek and places a hand on his shoulder.

'Boo!'

'Och, that got old a long time ago, Nikki,' Deek comments as he jumps in response to her touch and grabs for his gun where it's still hanging from his shoulder by the strap. 'Besides, I coulda shot ye.'

'I couldn't resist.' She flashes her pointed teeth at Deek. 'Besides, your bullets would not affect me.'

'Aye, well, what about a punch to the face?'

'Relax, there is nothing here, Deek,' she soothes.

'You quite sure because I'm getting the feeling we're being watched?' The feeling has persisted since we set foot in this place, and I'm not convinced by Nikki's assurances.

Nikki's crimson eyes roll in consternation. 'I was merely attempting to allay everybody's fear.'

'I fear nothing and no one,' Mist rebukes her.

'I was specifically referring to Deek.'

'Why me *specifically*? I can haundle maself.'

'Even if confronted with magical guardians?' she enquires playfully.

'Can we just take a minute?' I intercede before the situation escalates. 'What exactly did you find, Nikki?'

'A stone sarcophagus, undoubtedly the last resting place of that who we seek, resting upon a raised altarpiece. And these…'

She guides us towards a set of three steps that lead to a raised pathway. On either side are displayed two stone jackals, sitting obediently to attention on massive square stone plinths to accommodate their massive stone bodies. They're quite terrifying and not like any of the ones you may have seen before in ancient art. At least fifteen feet high — sitting down — but it's hard to tell from down here. Their muscles are well defined, the skeletal structure overdeveloped, protruding in places to form bony spikes at elbows and knees and a ridge along their spines. And their eyes seem to be fashioned out of faceted red jewels, their bared teeth moulded from gold.

'Och, they're only statues.' Deek reaches out to touch the plinth the nearest one is seated upon. 'But no very bonnie ones.'

'Don't,' Maddie warns, her commanding tone halting Deek's outstretched hand. 'They may not be as lifeless as they appear.'

'Guardians.'

I look over to Kal as she names them.

'Undoubtedly. I have fought similar constructs over the centuries conjured by dark wizards. We would do well to avoid such contrivances. Proceed with much caution, all of you,' she advises.

That's advice I'm definitely going to adhere to because if there's one thing Kal knows about, it's demon-slaying.

Those ruby-red eyes flicker as Sophia glides past the stone guardians giving the impression that their gaze is indeed tracking our movements.

The flaming troughs of oil have converged on this raised pathway and guide us towards our destination like lights on a runway.

'How was this place constructed?' Anastassia enquires. 'Or should I ask, how did you construct this place?'

'A combination of magic and mental projection, which as it is a power understood and wielded by the Nephilim could well amount to the same thing,' J tries to explain.

I've no better explanation, despite all our memories returning, it's still the small details that elude us.

'Created by thought alone,' Ix adds. 'Simply willing this place into existence.'

Now there's a thought. Quite literally!

Anastassia pauses in her step. Her military training, one which has kept her alive for so long, captures my attention. She's picked up on something.

Mist cocks her head as well. 'Movement,' she whispers, drawing her axe.

Deek has also unslung his automatic, and he turns to face whatever it is that has caught their attention, slowly releasing the safety as he does so. 'It's yon beasties, isn't it?'

I want to tell him not to be ridiculous, that they are only stone, and it's his imagination, but I can't because I know he's right.

'Sophia.' I whisper her name, and she immediately understands what's required and casts her light behind us.

Nikki, Maddie and Kal have all retraced their steps to join Mist and Anastassia, who were bringing up the rear of the pack. And I summon my power, ready to deliver a protective charm if required. But as these creatures were formed from magic themselves, I've no idea how effective my own enchantments will be against them. Maddie's talents as well may prove equally redundant, as I don't know if her gaze can ossify creatures already fashioned from stone.

I edge forward to what now is the front of the pack, J with me every step of the way. I can feel his psychic potential vibrating at a fantastic frequency as he readies himself. Even Ix is hovering in between forms, fading in and out like a photograph developing over and over.

The shadows are denser beyond Sophia's comforting nimbus, and I'm struggling to see anything. 'Nikki?'

'They're coming,' she confirms.

They! Great, we've got both to contend with.

I can hear their stone claws now, clicking on the floor, and I catch the glint of red eyes.

Kal draws two swords. A katana and her trusty demon slayer, as Deek shoulders his rifle and aims down the sights. But bullets, I feel, will do little to halt their progress.

'We must have triggered a magical charm when we passed them,' I whisper to J.

'Like your tripwires?'

'Yes, but these were cast by someone far more adept than me otherwise I would have sensed them.'

The shadows condense as the forms of the two jackal guardians loom into view, their front haunches low to the ground as they stalk us. A low menacing growl, like the distant rumble of thunder, vibrates through the floor, caressing the soles of my feet, and I see sharp teeth glinting — like golden daggers.

When the first one finally attacks, launching itself off the floor with powerful hind legs, I barely have time to react. It's Kal who moves first, swiftly inserting herself between this hound of hell and the rest of us.

Only now, as it enters the light, can we fully appreciate the full scale of these creatures, an incised glyph now glowing upon its chest — Nephthys' mark — which had lain dormant and unseen upon our earlier examination until she called upon its revival.

Kal side steps as the beast lunges, its teeth cracking together like the sound of a gunshot. She brings her demon slayer down with a powerful sweep of her arm, the stone splits cleanly, and the jackal's head falls to the ground with a resounding thud that fills the chamber with its echo. Mist takes up a stance as she prepares to engage the second beast.

'Wait!' I release J's hand and move forward. 'It's okay.' I reassure him. At least I hope it is, but I've got a strong feeling about this, and I edge forward, stretching out one hand.

'You sure you know what you are doing?' Mist asks as I edge past her.

'No.' I've got to be honest, but something is driving me on. This is about trust… it's a test. If this beast attacks now, then it will raise all sorts of questions regarding Nephthys' true intentions. It's something I've got to pursue; this is a pivotal moment for us all.

As I near the guardian, I find myself murmuring gentle crooning noises of encouragement and the jackal edges cautiously forward, its upright pointed ears swivelling in response to my reassurances before finally lying down and allowing me to approach and pet its massive snout.

I shall be perfectly honest with you, silent reader, my top is saturated with sweat right now, and my hair is plastered to my forehead. That was one of the scariest things I've ever done. Swimming with sharks — nothing! But now that I'm up close, I'm thinking a pack of these things would go a long way if it came to battling it out with the Nephilim. It could easily take off my whole arm with those jaws.

But my gut feeling was right. It recognises something in me, some magical trace that it connects with its mistress. And with a final tentative sniff of my hand, it melts back into the darkness to no doubt take up its position on the stone plinth once more in endless vigilance.

'You're totally mental, you know that?'

'People have commented on it over the years, Deek.'

J wraps me in a hug. 'Well done.'

I needed that.

'Very impressive, Alice.' Nikki commends me as she paces around the severed head.

'Now we know Nephthys' intentions are good.' Ix smiles.

Which is a bit weird because you can always see her teeth; funny I've never mentioned it before.

I join Nikki to study the head more closely before checking out the body. It's just stone as far as I can tell — the glowing glyph has completely disappeared now, indicating to me that the magic used to animate this creature has been withdrawn. A line from a film occurs to me as I study the massive body.

'I know a taxidermy man; he's gonna have a heart attack when he sees what I've brought him.' I grin round at my companions after I deliver them the line. Although now that I've spoken the words, I realise I've probably misquoted the line, but it's close enough.

Nothing. They just stare back at me blankly as if my encounter with the creature has shaken a couple of bolts loose inside my head.

114

'No? *Jaws*? Anybody?' It's completely wasted on them. I thought at least Deek would get it as it was something we got into the habit of when on the road to pass the time, quoting lines from films at appropriate moments for maximum comic effect. But this one fell flatter than a roadkill armadillo.

'Yeah, I think I remember it now,' J recalls, frowning as he tries to remember the scene to which I'm referring.

Not quite the response I was hoping for.

'Aye, I've seen the film, but I cannae mind the line though.'

'Well, it's in there, Deek. I've seen it loads of times.'

'Didnae say it wasn't; I just cannae mind it.'

'What is it about?' Maddie asks, her interest piqued.

'A big mad shark,' Deek says.

Hardly an accurate, critical overview of such an iconic movie.

'I don't like sharks,' Sophia confesses as she alights amongst us.

'How can you not like sharks? You're a divine being — surely all life is sacred to you?' I ask.

'It is. I just don't like them. It's their eyes. Or flies, or snakes, or mice…'

'Mice? Really?' Deek asks, surprised.

'Can we please stop discussing animal phobias?' I wish I'd never tried my *Jaws* line on them now. One

115

which I'd been saving for ages just for the right moment.

'They're not phobias; I just don't like them,' Sophia continues.

Have you ever needed to pinch the bridge of your nose, right between the eyebrows, and shake your head in despair? You know where I'm at right now then.

'I'm no a fan o' spiders,' Deek confesses.

They're still at it!

'Arachnids? You surprise me.' Anastassia raises her eyebrows. 'Back in my old home, the place was alive with spiders. It was a regular occurrence to be woken up with one running across your body or face in the dark.'

Deek's face is a pure picture. I don't think mine is much of an improvement after considering Anastassia's statement.

'I must have eaten many in my time whilst I was sleeping.'

I walk away, shaking my head; I don't want to hear any more. You'd never guess that this was the team that had already saved the human race once before.

'They are like children,' Kal says as she joins me. 'They mean no harm — they are merely expressing their emotions.'

'I know, I'm just nervous, I guess.'

'Pre-trip jitters,' J says. 'Don't sweat it — I'm the same.'

'It is a quite normal and rational reaction to what you are about to partake in,' Ix informs me. 'It is a good thing that they deal with their fears now — expose and confront them.'

Kal nods, fully understanding. 'Expressing their demons, as you did, when you approached and subdued the guardian.'

Cool. I'm feeling better now. Nothing like a hug from J and a few wise words of wisdom from Kal and Ix.

I tune back into the conversation the rest of the team are involved in a little distance behind us now, which has now progressed on to Marmite. Which I can't abide, but J is partial to it.

Ix leans in close to me and whispers, 'What is Marmite?'

'A yeasty spread.' When I put it like that, no wonder I don't like it.

'It sounds most unsavoury.'

Well, what do you say to that? It is unsavoury, to my palate at least, but then again, it is savoury!

What the hell are you talking about, Alice? You must be wondering the same. I need to give myself a shake and get back on track and focus. It's just stress that's causing me to trivialise.

'We are wasting time.' Kal is bored with listening to the pros and cons of Marmite, and she leads the march onwards.

The sarcophagus, when we reach it, is as impressive as any I've seen on-screen or in a book, despite its plainness. Meaning it isn't adorned with gold or lapis lazuli, the only addition being thin gold bands that encircle her eyes. The black stone has been carved into a lifelike effigy of the elusive Nephthys and catching sight of it for the first time gives me tingles.

The likeness lies reposed with her arms folded neatly across her chest, Egyptian style, her hair neatly braided and beaded in a style common for that era. The attention to detail is quite breathtaking. The plinth that supports the coffin is, like the walls and pillars, adorned with hieroglyphs, and it is positioned centrally within an eight-pointed star carved into the floor.

The significance of this number is not overlooked by any of us. This is a very auspicious event for us all, and I take a moment to fully assimilate the occasion and all it portends.

Kal lifts the lid of the sarcophagus easily with one hand, despite it weighing at least half a ton, and holding it up, she peers inside. 'It's empty.'

That doesn't surprise me. This is where we will perform the ceremony, and with silent synchronicity, we each take up a position, sitting or kneeling at a point of the star inscribed on the floor.

'What should we do?' Anastassia asks.

'Watch over us.' I shrug. There's very little else either she or Deek can do now; it's up to us.

'What if that other beastie comes back?'

'Throw it a biscuit?' Anastassia suggests.

'I dinnae have any biscuits on me.'

'I am joking. We will be fine. Alice has tamed the beast. We will be here when you return.' She reaches for Mist's hand and kisses it lightly. 'Stay safe.'

Ix lays the wrapped leaf before her and carefully unfolds it to reveal the shaved strands of bark. The thin slivers curl in on themselves like, what else? Wood shavings. She selects a piece and places it on her tongue before handing the package to Anastassia, as we are separated by several feet. 'If you would be so kind. Chew the bark thoroughly,' she advises, 'before swallowing.'

I accept the proffered leaf and pluck out the smallest piece, and pop it into my mouth before returning the unfurled leaf to Anastassia, who delivers it to J.

At first, it doesn't taste so bad, a bit astringent, like aspirin, but by the time Anastassia backs away, everyone now having partaken, I can detect an underlying and far more pungent, spicy flavour coming through. One which floods my mouth with saliva as my tongue starts to go numb, and bracing myself, I swallow the concoction, feeling my stomach flip as it threatens to reject the potion and my recently consumed takeaway. In retrospect, I would rather have been faced with consuming a slice of toast spread with Marmite.

For several minutes, nothing happens, then I become aware of a gentle rocking sensation, like sitting on the deck of a small boat. The sensation steadily strengthens, and I glance over at J, who's sat on my right, and he gives me a wink. Ix, who's on my left, gives me a gentle, reassuring nod of her head, and I feel myself relaxing more. Mist is positioned on Ix's left, and I can see Nikki on J's right. The massive stone sarcophagus blocks my view of the others, but Sophia's aura still casts sufficient light for me to still make out the details of my immediate companions. Soon though, even her comforting golden light begins to dim as Sophia succumbs to the effects of the bark, and the flickering flames that dance across the surface of the oil seem to recede into the distance casting us into darkness.

I focus my intent, recounting Kal's meditation techniques she has taught me, and I slow my breathing and empty my mind — which is far harder than it sounds. Soon coloured filaments brighten the inner darkness and dance like living things, capturing my attention.

There's no turning back now.

11

The experience that I will now relate to you was certainly enlightening and, at times, terrifying as I relinquished my grasp on this reality and fully immersed myself. So, strap yourself in because, from my perspective at least, it's a hell of a ride.

Firstly, I can feel my thoughts expanding as I'm poised on the very precipice of something monumental, like sitting in a rollercoaster car as it sits atop that first vertiginous peak, ready to take the plunge. Have you seen *Contact*? With Jodie Foster? Well, if you have, you'll remember the part when she travels through the wormholes as she's conveyed from one location to the next. That's the best description I can formulate for what happens next.

Colours of indescribable vibrance streak past and through me as my mind accelerates forward — or expands. I can't see the rest of my crew in this altered state, but I can feel them with me every step of the way. Later discussions did reveal that they did indeed all experience the same sensations as we journeyed together.

My anxiety begins to creep until I finally relent and let go of my subconscious fears, and I lose all sense of physicality — my body no longer exists, and I soar. I am no longer in control; I am at the complete mercy of this spirit plant now, and I am simultaneously exhilarated and petrified.

What I perceive to be stars rush by at phenomenal speeds, but all my previous conceptions of space and time are shattered — they bear no relevance any more — they are merely concepts that humankind abide by.

Give me a copy of *A Brief History of Time* right now, and I reckon I'd grasp far more than three per cent of what Professor Hawking was writing about.

I now find myself within a different reality, dimension. Inhabited by beings of pure energy, their world beyond my capacity to describe with any degree of accuracy. I can only watch on with child-like fascination, rapt and in awe.

Then I sense, rather than see, conflict — there is now disharmony saturating this place. A secondary race, one that I can immediately relate to, then come into focus. Giants — tall, beautiful, godly — Titans of myth and legend. And others, although similar but smaller in stature, which I liken to the ancient gods of Olympus revered by the Ancient Greeks. Beings such as we have encountered before and slain. The remnants of a once mighty and proud race.

The aftermath of this aeon spanning conflict between these three races once more sees me arrive back within an environment that I recognise — Earth. But during a period in prehistory, now long forgotten, all traces of the first civilisations I now witness built upon the foundations of their ancient predecessors rise from the ashes like the mythical phoenix. The events I'm witnessing then begin to slow as we enter the age of the great Egyptian civilisations. I am standing within a group of eight. The number is not lost to me even in this altered condition. We are gathered within a tomb, the very tomb, in fact, that our physical bodies now inhabit.

I sense a coming storm, not an elemental one, but a spiritual collision, and we have gathered here in mutual consent to lay our ninth member to rest. Although all in attendance are cloaked and hooded, I do not need to see their faces to know who they are. The ritual concludes, my mind remembering that Nephthys is a renegade such as us, a pariah of her people. We have all forsaken and cast aside former beliefs, teachers and religious systems we no longer believe in and, therefore, no longer adhere to. We have formed our own clandestine ennead. We have witnessed much in the subjugation of the peoples of Earth, the lesser species. The atrocities we have seen, the acts of violence committed, the endless horrors. We have made a stand, and we unite, planning for the future, but first, we must forget.

The energy is dense, like fog. The magic's powerful and venerable, and I remember it all. I recall other traits attributed to the goddess Nephthys; that of protection and embalming — the preservation of a body, both physical and metaphysical, by employing methods of genetic dispersal. Mummification itself, as practised by the Egyptians — a simple endeavour to emulate the powers wielded by their gods. Like children sketching with crayons in an attempt to forge the works of the great masters.

I witness Nephthys' body unravel before my very eyes and disperse throughout Earth's creative sphere. This is an event we have all agreed upon. It is the only hope we have for our continued survival, vowing that in Earth's future, we will once more be united and conclude what we have already begun. To usurp those gods who have for centuries untold interfered and laid to waste civilisations throughout not just this world but countless others scattered throughout the universe. We are the chosen few who have taken on that burden, entrusted with a monumental task no others thought achievable. To guide humanity onwards to greater heights.

The Olympian gods stand glorious, for now, against the might of the Titans and Nephilim. Casting down the former and repelling the latter. But those victorious beings who remain now seek us out with the intention of annihilating the remaining threat to their continued reign.

In a bid to evade and survive their wrath, I, and one other, forfeit our lives after the dissemination of our luminary. A person who inspires others with regards to specific spheres of knowledge. For that was who Nephthys was to us all — our guiding light. The rest of our ennead is seized and imprisoned, but it was all part of our strategy.

My last conscious act was to place an object upon her breast. I recognise this object as Nephthys unravels into infinity.

Now I'm speeding forwards through time. Events flash across my sight at a rate I can hardly comprehend.

Reminiscent of the 1960s version of *The Time Machine* when the traveller collapses over the controls and plummets into the future.

Much of what I witness is almost instantaneously lost to me. Some more prominent places, people and past lives adhere. Perhaps lives in which myself and the other member of our ennead who maintained freedom crossed paths with me throughout the centuries.

I retain memories of serving as a priestess to the Delphic Oracle in Ancient Greece; I am a concubine to a Roman general during the final years of the Empire; I can see bison amassing in their thousands as they migrate across vast savannahs before the advent of the white man; I feel the rising flames as I'm burnt at the stake for practising herbalism, and I recognise some of the jeering faces in the crowd, all they are missing are homemade placards with printed slogans upon them; a Victorian governess who falls foul of consumption.

I recall so much…

The heady rush and reminiscence through time slows, and I'm myself, almost. I inhabit the body from my previous life. My sister, Emily, has not long departed, and I'm alone. Was Nephthys present in some aspect of Emily? Watching over me? Some aspect of myself tells me it is true.

My diligence and ability have ensured my financial stability at this cardinal point in my advancement, amassing a substantial fortune across numerous accounts. This knowledge becomes known to me — something profound is soon to occur within this lifetime. But right now, it all means nothing to me; I'm in mourning.

London.

I wander aimlessly. I remember the sun warming my skin, a small shop tucked away in a side street somewhere. I take a moment and close my eyes, bathing in the warmth and light, as harassed shoppers step around me, muttering under their breath. A cool breeze kisses my cheek lightly, and I open my eyes and enter the shop. I'm drawn to a particular crystal. It is of the common variety, but the fracture inside catches the light when I pick it up, and the rainbow structure reminds me of a winking eye as I turn it back and forth. It makes me smile, and I purchase it. Now I know that this is the same crystal I had placed upon the breast of Nephthys.

A remembrance lest we forget.

I feel as though I'm falling now from a great height, the memory I have just relived dwindling into obscurity. The final piece of the puzzle has now found its correct place. I panic for a split second until I realise that I'm back inhabiting my physical body. The sensation of falling persists until I pick out the denser shadows of J and Ix on either side of me, and I relax and reacquaint myself with the physical world.

I'm aware of my breath as I slowly inhale and exhale, my chest rising and falling, and the fact that my legs are completely numb from sitting cross-legged. Sophia's light casts its warmth on the other side of the sarcophagus, and it quickly strengthens and expands as she fully regains cognisance.

We all sit for a few minutes as we readjust, as I try to recall how to work this fleshy avatar I inhabit. I finally turn my head, and J's smile warms my heart and grounds me further.

I grimace as I stretch my legs; the pain of the blood rushing back shoots pins and needles the full length of both limbs. But I know that we aren't finished yet, as do the others, who remain seated in position.

I know what to do. I always did. I possessed the power and had unknowingly been carrying the catalyst around with me for years. Its presence so much a part of me it had become second nature to pick it up and place it in my pocket each morning, as you would your mobile phone or house keys when leaving home. I'd never even considered its significance until now. An item bought on a whim. A crystal that entered my life once more, manipulated by Nephthys to jumpstart my memories and reform the ennead. Burying it beneath an ancient Yew located in a churchyard in Greenwich late in my then life, and unearthing it once more in this one, the exact site ingrained firmly in my memory.

I can stand now, my legs still tingling, and Kal and Nikki, acting in perfect harmony, come to my aid and lift the heavy stone lid off the sarcophagus and lower it to the ground before once more taking up their respective positions.

The tingling is more than just a result of my protracted period of sitting cross-legged as I dip into my pocket and retrieve the stone. Its faceted surfaces warm in my hand, the vibrational energy filling my whole being. I smile as I place the stone within the exposed cavity as a trace of Sophia's light is refracted, and the rainbow eye winks up at me, repeating the process I performed on this very spot centuries before.

My breath catches as I detect a faint pulse of light within the lattice of the stone, one which carries a steady beat — a heartbeat. The darkness that abides within the coffin is suddenly filling with iridescent threads, called back through aeons of time, each one encoded with the memory of who they once were. I watch, mesmerised, as they weave together, increasing in momentum as the framework fabricates.

I see a skeletal structure forming, a circulatory system, musculature, organs, skin, all woven together from vibrant, colourful threads of life, each one imbued with the gift of remembrance.

I see eyes sparkling brimming with intelligence, hazel-tinted and warm as they stare up into my own, and

I perceive recognition and friendship. My own eyes fill with tears, my vision blurring as the form completes its reconstruction, the rainbow weave fading to be replaced by brown skin and dark, plaited, beaded hair. I'm overwhelmed with emotion as our mentor, the matriarchal figure within our group is returned to us, and I remember... I remember it all as if it were only yesterday.

I reach out as she reaches out to me, and I feel the soft warmth of her hand against my palm as we make contact.

'Welcome back.'

12

Wow! How intense was that, right? Ancient god-like beings and a rebel alliance — what does that remind you of?

You might want to take five and grab a tea or a coffee or something? And some chocolate, I know I could go some right about now. I am still feeling a bit shaky — physically and emotionally.

Kal has just read my condition and has tossed me over a chocolate bar she had stashed in her cargo pants. She's a complete star.

'I don't suppose you've got a flask of tea in there as well, have you?' I'll admit I'm pushing my luck now.

'No, but will this do?'

She retrieves a bottle of water from another pocket and passes it over, and I accept it gratefully. I offer some chocolate to J, who waves it off — I'm kind of glad I need the sugar — but he accepts some water. It's warm, but right now, I don't care.

We're all still a bit spaced out and overawed in the presence of Nephthys, who, with a hand from me, has climbed out of her stone repose and is once more standing amongst us.

I can't even begin putting into words what I'm feeling right now. But now that she is returned to us, I do not doubt that the repercussions of such an accomplishment will soon become very apparent. But as we're not faced with a deranged deity or power-hungry god, she is truly one of us, I can't help but grin. Dark-skinned and beautiful, she surveys us in turn, clothed in the same Egyptian shift she was dispersed in.

She raises delicate fingers and touches the skin of her face reverently, as if unconvinced yet of her return to physicality. Small patches of skin and hair blur and colour, small threads swaying gently along her contours periodically before being withdrawn. Either this is a symptom of the magic she regulates, or her physical body is still getting accustomed to being flawless and intact. I can't be sure, and I can't begin to imagine what is going through her mind right now.

Unsurprisingly, it's Deek who first breaches the silence. 'So, all went according to plan then? This is Nephthys?'

He actually got her name right this time! I'm impressed.

'That was a name which I was known by, yes,' she answers, her voice barely a whisper.

'Awesome.'

I can't argue with that, Deek.

'Took you long enough.'

I draw my attention away from the team to fully confront Deek. 'What do you mean? How long were we out?'

'A little over eight hours,' Anastassia informs me. 'You slept through most of it.' She prods Deek with a finger accusingly.

'I couldnae help it. It's so dark in here, and I was bored,' he says rather guiltily.

'I must confess I also succumbed for a time,' Anastassia reveals. 'I had strange dreams... of other times and different places,' she muses thoughtfully.

So, she at least was swept up with us to an extent, which doesn't surprise me — that was a very powerful event. But eight hours! I would have guessed at about an hour or so at most.

'What about you, Deek? You pick up on anything?'

'No, nothing. I slept like the dead. No pun intended.'

'Introduce me, sister, to your friends,' Nephthys requests, joining us. Her voice has now gained strength, her accent soft and husky, bestowing a certain sense of peace within me.

'This is Anastassia and Deek, good friends to us. They've both proved invaluable in our previous pursuits.'

'It is an honour to meet you both,' she defers.

'Likewise,' says Deek.

Anastassia dips her head in respect.

'Much has progressed since last we were together,' she says to me.

She takes the time again to fully take us all in, her smile a joy to behold. Finally, she reaches out to me with both hands, and I take them in my own.

'And you, my apprentice, my sister. You were tasked with such a heavy burden, but you prevailed as I knew you would. I can still barely believe that, once more, I stand amongst you all. Is this a dream created by my weary mind? A hallucination taunting me across aeons of time?' She laughs — the sound is quite magical. 'But no, my sister, Isis, it is truly you.'

I'm going to use a phrase Deek has used before that adequately describes what I'm thinking and feeling at this precise moment — holy shit!

One of my previous incarnations was that of Isis herself! I can barely believe that. Obviously, because of Nephthys' origins, we're not sisters in the true sense of the word. Maybe she even concocted the personage of Nephthys specifically to make contact with me and the others to draw us together and impart her wisdom and knowledge — but still, Isis!

That's one in the eye for all those spiritual types who have proclaimed to have been Isis in a past life. Wrong, it was me! I have just had it confirmed by a very reliable source.

Wait... perhaps I'm thinking of Cleopatra?

'Married yourself a real-life goddess.' I step closer to J and nudge him with my hip in what I hope is a demurely goddess-like fashion.

'I already knew you were a goddess.'

Right answer, but I'm glad it's still relatively dark, as I can feel a blush burning my cheeks.

'And my magi.' Nephthys now turns her attention to J. 'Faithful to the end.'

'It's Jackson now.'

I'm going to have to quiz J later about his past lives — that could be very interesting.

She smiles radiantly. 'All of you.' She casts her gaze over the gathering. 'Many of you have suffered so much, and for that, I will be filled with regret eternally.' She rests a hand over her heart. 'But the joy that suffuses me as I stand before you all again. I am your humble servant.'

As my software has been fully updated — so to speak — so has that of the rest of the team, and there is very little need for further words; the expressions on everybody's faces speak volumes. We just all... know.

'Did you hear that?' Anastassia asks.

And I did, like a bomb detonating on the surface of the sands far in the distance. A second boom follows seconds later, followed by a drizzle of sand as it drifts down from the ceiling.

'Surely naw the military?' Deek questions looking up.

'They have located me,' Nephthys elucidates, and there is no need for her to name to who she refers.

Another boom sounds directly above us, the ominous sound resonating within the cavernous chamber, and seconds later, more sand sprinkles down from above.

'Are we gonna be safe doon here?'

Nephthys cocks her head as she considers Deek's words. 'Your tongue is strange. I am not familiar with your people.'

'Scottish, ma'am.'

Ma'am! Get Deek.

She ponders this for a moment before answering. 'Born of noble, warrior stock.'

'Aye, that's me.'

'Yes, my noble warrior, this place is sealed with ancient charms.'

Noble warrior! She'll be giving him visions of grandeur.

Another boom fills the room. That rhymed, sorry, a consequence of writing songs for the band; sometimes I just can't help myself.

'But the stone is ancient, weakened by the passage of centuries,' she considers. 'It may well fracture and crumble under persistent attack.'

'Should we leave then?'

'You, my child,' she addresses Anastassia, 'you have a strong heart, trustworthy, and have endured much hardship, a fine companion for my Valkyrie warrior.'

Nephthys certainly doesn't seem to be too concerned at the arrival of the Nephilim above us, and judging by the sound of it, there must be at least a dozen up there. And now their prize has manifested, they're gathering like eager shoppers awaiting the doors being flung open on the first day of the sales. And they won't be leaving until they've snapped up a bargain.

'We have time enough in hand to deal with their threat.' She allays Anastassia's fears. 'They are not what they once were; their power has diminished over the millennia. All things eventually age and die, and they cling to life like ticks on a dog.'

'So, you've got a plan, then?' I ask, buoyed up by the prospect.

Nephthys smiles, and I'm suddenly aware that everything is going to be all right. She traces a delicate glyph in the air with her fingers, and the sarcophagus lid responds, resealing the stone coffin she was entombed in. Well, not entombed in exactly. J, being the science fiction fan, later likened the coffin as a, now let's see if I get this right — a phase harmonic teleportation device — there. Then that means all those glyphs inscribed on its surface act a bit like microcircuitry. I've been so used to referring to the potential I draw upon as 'magic' I'm still struggling to get my head around the fact that it is, in reality, just a branch of alien science that has been far beyond our capacity to fully comprehend. I'm just going to keep on referring to it as magic.

Nephthys seats herself upon the now repositioned sarcophagus lid and beckons to us to be seated once more. I can't even recall her moving, which is something I more fully take in, later on, the way she travels through the physical world; I'll share with you then.

We comply as Anastassia and Deek step back into the shadows once more, accompanied by a further two booms from overhead, and I hear the gentle patter of sand as it dusts the floor.

Nephthys leads us on this second excursion, but our combined energy is still vibrating at a high frequency, and within a few short, guided breaths, we merge as one entity, completely synchronised.

I lower my eyelids and this time the experience reminds me of a different fairground ride. Funny that — maybe we construct these 'entertainments' to subconsciously attempt to experience or revive some ancient revenant that is an inherent part of us all. Maybe not. Maybe we just like being thrilled and shaken up after a couple of beers. Besides, I can't think of anything profound and spiritual about rubber dingy rapids! I can't remember the name of this particular ride — gravity wall — or something. The one where you are pinned to the interior wall of a large drum, and you're spun around at such a rate that when the floor drops away, you remain stuck to the inside — that one!

13

Consequently, I feel as though the world has dropped away from under me, and I'm suspended in a vacuum and contradictorily feel like I've been fired from a cannon — more funfair comparisons — no wait, that's circuses. Strange how these 'trips' or altered state journeys have countless opposing perceptions super-imposed on each other. Soon the sensation fades away, and I'm weightless, or that's how it feels, as if I'm floating in space, but I can breathe… but I don't need to breathe, do I? Am I breathing?

Pull yourself together, Alice.

'You can open your eyes,' Nephthys communicates to us.

Whether via thought or speech, I can't be sure, but I consent, and I immediately comprehend why I'm feeling the way I am.

No longer do we inhabit that dark repository. The thunderous booms of the Nephilim as they attempt to gain entry into our sanctuary are also no longer in evidence. We are here, together, suspended in space. Gone also is the sarcophagus, and I can clearly see each member of the team, but of Nephthys, there is no sign. Instead, slowly rotating at our centre is a perfect miniature of the Earth, down to the last snow-peaked cap, delicate swirl of cloud and tract of dense forest.

'I am with you now.' Her voice resounds strongly within the group. 'In every fibre, every atom, every breath of wind and drop of moisture. My Ka—'

Not as in the small car, but in Ancient Egypt, it was the spiritual essence of a human or indeed a god.

'—suffuses all. I have immersed myself completely to evade those who seek to reclaim me, now as I did centuries ago. My bond with this world is ineffable, as is the bond we share within our ennead.'

And as I study our blue planet, I'm coming to believe more and more that this version is the real Earth and not a facsimile, and we've somehow achieved god-like status and are suspended in space somehow. Was this what we had always been destined for? Had the time of the old gods finally drawn to a close? Was our combined destiny now to carry that mantle? Overseers of the Earth, tasked with its continued protection.

Now that I focus, I can begin to make out tiny details: a spiral of cloud that could indicate a gathering storm that very much resembles an eye; an archipelago of islands that, from this elevation, reminds me of a long, delicately curved finger; a rainforest, the tightly compacted trees looking to me like strands of braided hair; a chain of snow-capped mountains resembles a flash of perfect teeth. The comparisons go on and on the more I really look. I see the sweep of her neck, the tone of her skin, the ripples of her shift...

Everywhere I looked, I saw a resemblance, and I understood… as did we all. By saving our sister, reforming our ennead, our group of nine, we had been given the opportunity to save so much more.

I feel now as if I'm being pulled backwards and forwards through time simultaneously. I don't think they've got one of those at the funfair yet. This time I feel euphoric; I have nothing to fear. The globe of the Earth is still suspended within the centre of our group, but it is now trailing smaller spheres in its wake as they plummet into infinity. A soft laugh escapes my lips as I realise what we are doing, what we are achieving — we Pariahs.

Despite the others having little dialogue at this juncture in our story, it is simply because we have been all experiencing the very same thing. The only previous discrepancies were my and J's past lives recollections as the rest of the team had been immured during this long period in our existence. Which, I'm glad to inform you, when I asked Sophia about this, that they experienced a sharing of my own and J's existences. Which was a big relief otherwise that would have been a seriously bad trip for the rest of the crew. Ix as well was spared from reliving her time in that concocted underworld, subjugated to the will of Her.

I realised now that we had only been hunted by those ancient gods out of fear, like a dying person clutching desperately to life rather than relinquishing their hold and moving on. We were a very real threat to their continued reign, and they sensed our power, perhaps even foresaw what was to befall them. The nine of us, guided by Nephthys, had freed ourselves from the constraints of centuries, and we now held the power to bestow that same gift to others... when they were ready. We had forged a new future, no doubt aided along the way by countless friends and strangers, fleeting acquaintances, chance meetings, all kindled by our ever-vigilant Nephthys. Much of the time, I doubt she even consciously realised what she was doing, so finely dispersed was she throughout creation, as she hid in plain sight.

To sum up this whole concept, this plan of ours that had been nurtured and implemented so long ago, in a word, it was — exquisite. Maybe in many ways, that in itself is the pure essence of magic after all.

14

An appropriate analogy has just occurred to me, which I will share with you in a moment. And don't stray too far, my ardent bibliophile, as the action is far from over, despite, as will now be apparent, if you've still got your television switched on in the background, the threat of the Nephilim has been categorically erased from the world — permanently.

But it wasn't actually until Deek, with his brusque Scottish observation, brought home to me the result of our combined action as we stood gathered like some old school gang reminiscing at a school reunion. But without having to indulge in conversation with people you never liked or even bullied you during your youthful years.

'It sounds like they metal bampots have gone.'

And it was only then that I realised that the ominous booming, a result of the Nephilim attempting to breach our sanctuary, had ceased.

'Their time has passed,' Nephthys confirmed.

'Sweet,' he replied, grinning. 'Now that does call for a drink.'

'But how did you achieve such a victory?' Anastassia asks far more pragmatically.

'Together, we created infinite versions of the Earth, drawing the Nephilim into alternate versions of this planet, whilst I held their physical constructs firmly in this realm. Then the surrogate Earths were wiped from existence carrying the Nephilim into oblivion.'

'Aye?' Deek responded. 'Just like that?'

'Just like that,' Nephthys replied.

'Like pulling snails from their shells,' J surmised.

Nephthys dipped her head, acknowledging his comparison to what we had incredibly pulled off.

'So, all their armour is still lying up there?' Deek indicated with a tilt of his chin.

I knew exactly what he was thinking. 'You're not putting anything on eBay.'

'Course not. I was just thinking about a wee souvenir, that's all.'

'Didn't you see the size of those things? What did you plan on doing with it?'

'Dinnae ken.' He shrugs. 'Hadn't really thought that far ahead. Maybe just a foot? Make a nice planter for my ma.'

The most advanced civilisation humankind had yet encountered, and Deek's thinking about turning it into a flowerpot!

'Then we should leave this place.' Mist speaks up now that the threat has been lifted.

But where to? Our home in Canada will no doubt be overrun with soldiers, which only left New York as an option, but that wasn't an alternative I was going to be content with for very long.

'But first, before we withdraw...' Nephthys approaches Maddie and reaches for her shades.

Maddie flinches in response to her action, she only removes her shades when in conflict situations, and we are both aware of the consequences of such an act.

'Do not fear, child. You have no need of these spectacles.' And with a delicate touch, she slides the glasses off her face and hands them to her. 'You never did require them. You have complete mastery of your gift; you merely lacked the confidence and belief in yourself.'

And Nephthys is right. Even within the period I've known Maddie, her control over her ossifying stare has certainly become more disciplined and focused.

Maddie blinks a few times as she hooks her now redundant shades into her top and takes each one of us in with her sight.

And we're all still here in living flesh, no statues.

And wow, she's got the most amazing emerald eyes, ones that certainly benefit from not being hidden behind mirrored lenses.

'I can still feel my power, but... yes, the control I now possess...' She turns back to Nephthys, her eyes misty with tears. 'Thank you.'

'You have no need to thank me; it is far less than you deserve.'

Next, she turns to Nikki. 'Nyx, my queen of the night, so long have you been at the mercy of the one who cursed you. But no longer.' She steps in close and gently places a kiss upon her forehead, her palms resting lightly on either cheek, before stepping back.

Nikki also blinks a few times, this time out of surprise.

'How do you feel?' I'm curious as she still maintains her crimson eyes and serrated teeth, although I'm convinced she is very proud of these unique features and would be reluctant to lose them. They are very her, I have to admit, and it would've taken some getting used to. But, now that I think about it, perhaps those features were always a part of her physical makeup even before the curse was bestowed. I'd never considered this possibility until now.

'Yes,' she breathes. 'I feel… released.'

'So, no more nights out for you?' Deek comments.

'Not in that respect, no. But I will still drink you under the table.'

'Aye, no doubt.'

It's strange, even though the team generally look to me for guidance most of the time, I'd always seen Nikki as the elder of our little group. But now that Nephthys is fully present, it is she who has taken upon the role of matriarch, a role which she was always destined to fill.

Oh yes, I almost forgot that analogy I referred to ages ago. The eight of us have all got very intrinsic roles to play in our band. Whether actively involved with the playing of an instrument, singing or a more behind-the-scenes participation — stage show, management and marketing. All of which is an essential part of maintaining a band whilst on and off the road. And now Nephthys has returned, I see her fitting right in; it's as if that slot has just been waiting for her to fill it. I see her as the one that sits in the mixing room, adjusting and tweaking and enhancing our sound to musical perfection. Not quite literally, you understand, but I feel, with her presence, we have just been brought into sharper focus, so much so it's hard to believe that we have managed so long without her. Or did we? She's probably been a very real presence, an invisible hand guiding and protecting us along the way.

I glance down at those long, elegant fingers. Our band certainly could benefit from the addition of a keyboard player. But now's not the time.

I'm aghast and deeply moved to witness Nikki, who was very much private when it came to emotions — between you and me, for a long time I wondered if she even had any in the same sense as you or I do — throw her arms around Nephthys, delivering her a hug, which was quite something to behold. It was a sight to warm the heart.

But now, it was finally time to vacate this place, and I was quite content to let Nephthys lead the way. I imagine she was quite keen to experience the world outside this place again, at least in her current form. And the stone wall that blocked our exit was swept aside with a cast of her hand and just as casually resealed behind us.

Our lengthy sojourn underground meant that when we resurfaced — all those steps again made me wish I'd just portaled everybody up here — the sun was in ascendence.

'Och, now it's roastin',' Deek exclaimed, ripping off his top.

That was an understatement — it was like stepping onto the surface of the sun. Don't exaggerate, Alice. Okay, it wasn't really otherwise we'd all be vaporised, but it is pretty hot. And since we last walked these sands, there are now a couple of new additions — the Nephilim.

Deek is first to scurry over, no doubt with the intention of pulling a piece of the armour off.

Kal prods the nearest collapsed exoskeleton with the toe of her boot before peering into the dark hollows of the eyes. 'An empty shell, nothing more.'

But still, seeing it here like this is quite intimidating.

Nikki casually pulls off the bright yellow metallic head and playfully tosses it towards Deek, who skips aside as it thuds onto the sand.

'Hey!'

'A souvenir.'

'He's not bringing that home.' I'm putting my foot down. Besides, it's massive; there would certainly be no room for it in the New York apartment.

A little distance away, another lies face down in the sand; this one is metallic green.

Sophia takes to the wing to survey the immediate area and spins around above us. 'There must be at least two dozen, possibly more.'

Although I'm super keen to leave this place and escape the heat, I clamber to the top of the dune to view the fruits of our labour, so to speak. And Sophia's right. The sand is littered with rainbow giants, looking like a set from a psychedelic science fiction movie. The greens, maroons, golds and violets glowing brightly in the intense light. Most are lying prone in the sand, but a few remain upright, like sentinels, and we can now see the efforts of their labours as they tried to penetrate the cavern below. Large craters litter the site, some appearing to reach a depth of thirty or forty feet.

And then it occurs to me as I survey the scene. It looks like a giant's sandpit, and the children have rushed off for their tea, leaving their impressive collection of multi-coloured robots behind. And unless these remnants are located by a passing spy satellite and retrieved, they will undoubtedly be buried beneath the drifting sands. But once the military have scooped up all the others, which is an aspect of our victory we can do little to prevent, then I'm quite sure armies of experts will turn up to excavate these specimens as well.

'You know what awaits.' Ix speaks up for the first time since Nephthys' arrival.

I know exactly what she is referring to, as does Nephthys.

'The gateway beckons,' she sighs.

But before we take the plunge, we still have a couple of loose ends to tie up.

'We should retrieve the master recordings of our new album,' Maddie reminds us, her verdant eyes glinting in the sun.

That's going to take some time to get used to.

Although we'd tested out a few new tunes at Glastonbury, we still had the full album stored back in the studio, and I was damned if I was going to allow some general or other to get his hands on it. Maddie had had the same thought.

'Yes, I believe that is some of our finest work,' Sophia agrees.

'Your musical band? Yes?' Nephthys asks.

'Pariahs,' Sophia answers.

'How very appropriate.'

'Then we are all in accord?' Mist enquires.

And despite what is lying in wait for us, we are.

'Rock 'n' roll.' Deek punches the air. 'I was thinkin'.'

'What?' I'm always filled with a little trepidation when Deek has that specific tone of voice, as many of the 'pranks' that transpired whilst on tour began with those very words.

'How about addin' a couple o' bonus tracks? You know, live recordings?'

Not a bad idea at all. We always like to throw in the odd cover version on stage. As I mentioned before, the more mature attendees, in particular, get fired up when they hear these numbers, pumping up the whole crowd.

'We will leave the details in your capable hands,' J answers, also warming to the idea.

It's not until I hear those words that I fully accept that we won't be around to involve ourselves or see the release of the completed product. It's a big blow but at the same time a natural progression, something that at least Nephthys foresaw, hence the advent of that new portal — it was our way out, our next evolutionary step.

'What do you mean?' Deek asks J. 'You'll be involved, right?'

'Our time here is almost concluded,' Sophia explains, landing at his side. 'It is time for us to move on.'

'And up,' J adds.

'What?' Deek glances to the sky. 'You mean out there? Like in a galaxy, far, far away?'

I can't help but smile at his movie reference. 'No, not quite.'

'We will never be far removed from this world,' Nephthys interjects. 'You may accompany us if you wish.'

I didn't expect that. But of course, he's welcome; he's as much a part of the team as any of the others and seeing Mist and Anastassia standing hand in hand, I had no doubts that they would both be accompanying us.

'I dinnae ken.' He frowns as he contemplates the offer and all it would entail.

'Perhaps we should show him?' Nephthys suggests.

Ix nods in agreement. 'Yes.'

'Show me what?'

'You'll see.' I smile.

And that he did.

15

After initially being completely overawed by the scene that unfolded as Ix led us into the plain between realms and thrusting his hand through the head of one of the recently departed — with no ill effects, I hasten to add — and calling over to me: 'Hey, Alice, look, I can see dead people!'

Yeah, good one, Deek, nice movie reference, but I'm not even acknowledging this one as he hadn't laughed at my earlier *Jaws* quote, so I just shrug and shake my head.

Once he calmed himself somewhat, Ix took him aside and educated him as to what this place represented and the choices it held for those recently departed. For the record, he could see the round portal through which the rest of us were soon to be departed ourselves, but not the three others the deceased milled before. It just wasn't his time yet.

Ix took him to sit beneath the nearest iridescent leafed tree, only their heads visible above the swaying grasses whilst the rest of us contemplated the newly woven portal and the view beyond. Which was now fully completed. The world that now confronted us was… sublime.

I can sense your disappointment at my rather inadequate portrayal, but I genuinely have no words that effectively describe what I'm seeing right now. You'll just have to apply your imagination, but I doubt even your best conjuration could come close to filling in the blanks. That's no condemnation of your own inherent skills, you understand, as I doubt any of us present here could have foreseen what lies in wait. Besides, it does feel deeply personal; this is solely for us Pariahs, a haven where we will no longer be hounded and persecuted by the military and confronted by zealots brandishing placards.

I've got to confess I am a little excited now.

Which was, to put it mildly from Deek's perspective when he first set foot in this place. He reminded me of a five-year-old who had just crept down the stairs on Christmas morning and seen all the neatly wrapped presents tucked beneath the Christmas tree.

Overall, it was a very magical experience for all of us. There was just one thing that was dialling up my anxiety, one which Anastassia brought to the fore after standing in awe for quite some time staring at her newly returned arm. Her prosthetic was gone and had been replaced by the original — I think it was the original at least, despite having been chewed up by a monster. I suspect when we return to Canada, the prosthetic will be in full effect once more, but it's comforting to know that when we finally depart, she will be wholly herself again. I did half expect Nephthys to step forth and restore her arm earlier, after working her magic on Maddie and, in particular, Nikki. But perhaps the growing back of limbs is beyond her capacity to achieve. Although I doubt that, it is more likely that she foresaw the limb restoration in this between place.

Anastassia couldn't quite believe it at first as she stood there clenching and unclenching her fist, wiggling her fingers and rolling her sleeve up to check that it wasn't just her hand that had been restored to her.

'And do you plan on tackling the military when we return?' she asked, still glancing down at her arm as if to check it hadn't miraculously resorted back.

'Is this something we should be concerned about?' Nephthys asked in a tone that suggested that we shouldn't be.

'We should at least be prepared,' J states. 'They will be well "dug in" by now, and even though the threat the Nephilim presented has been lifted, I don't think these guys are going to just pack up and leave. I think our last encounter fully revealed what they intended for us.'

'To subvert and contain us,' Kal concludes.

'Then we will have no alternative but to cut them down to size,' Mist states simply.

Maddie nods in agreement. 'I, too, have had my fill of these toy soldiers.'

She's donned her shades again, although she doesn't need them any more — they're so much a part of her dress code now, and I've got to admit they do look cool. But it is a shame to mask those beautiful eyes of hers.

'It may be that they will reconsider after witnessing the fall of the Nephilim. Perhaps they will be more open to negotiations now?'

What? I didn't expect this from Nikki, and I'm rather taken aback as, generally, her opinion of the average mortal is one of barely suppressed contempt. This new change in attitude can have only come as a result of her aeons old curse having been lifted, unlocking within her a more compassionate and empathic side to her nature.

'Perhaps?' Kal doesn't sound convinced.

'Then we will crush them.'

Ah, there we go, that's the Nikki I know.

'They will never cease in their harassment of us; it is not in their nature to forgive. They exist to subjugate and control, and we are an irritant to them, a scratch they have been unable to itch. They will continue to formulate ever more complex and intuitive schemes with which to ensnare and contain us.'

I've got to sadly admit that I'm with Sophia on that score. Who am I to argue with an angel anyway?

'We have no need to tread lightly; our ennead is unparalleled in their world. The magic we have at our beckoning will aid our cause.'

Not sure whether Nephthys is referring to Nikki's crush-them-before-our-might attitude or not? I think not, though, not if we can possibly do this peacefully.

Which does get me thinking, is this really worth it? For a few CDs? It does seem a bit extreme now that I think about it.

'I just wish to be freed from their darker nature, their repugnant thoughts.'

Sophia isn't finished yet. She's not talking about you, by the way; I'm quite sure your thoughts are charming and sweet, at least most of the time. But due to her unearthly beauty, she does attract unwanted attention quite regularly.

'I have witnessed much since my sojourn within the Earth realm, and much of what I have experienced saddens me. I am amongst friends here' — she brightens — 'and wish to remain so and take the next step of our journey together, as one.'

I hear what she's saying. She's only concerned that some of us may fall foul of these soldiers when we return. Then we'll just have to make sure that doesn't happen.

'But if you all insist on returning, then I will accompany you, and if we are met with violence, then they will also be met with the same.'

'We will hasten their arrival to this place of the newly dead.' Mist adds her slant to Sophia's words.

I've got to admit I prefer Sophia's speech, although they both amount to the same thing.

I sigh deeply. I'm loathed to resort to violence and have always sought a better alternative where possible. And it's ironic that after everything that we've faced, the demons we've vanquished and the deities we've cast down so everyone can sleep easier in their beds each night, that we're still hunted and feared by certain factions. I'm one step away from stepping up beside Mist and leading the charge. I'm tired of living my life wondering when a crack commando team is going to drop in unannounced, the skies above our home filled with helicopters. I worry about my friends, my husband, and along with Anastassia and Deek, J and I are still essentially mortal, the same as you. And they'll never stop; the tasering was just the beginning… they crossed the line.

'The most infernal demons are those garbed in human form,' Kal imparts.

And do you know what? There was never a truer word spoken.

'Are you sure you want to go through with this?' J asks me, although I know he's on the same page as me.

'Yeah, you?'

'You kidding?' He grins boyishly. 'That's the best album you've made. You can't just let that slip by. Think of the fans, what they'd be missing out on.'

When I hear it put like that… And I have been considering Deek as well. I do have a satchel of cash stashed in the house. It's been there for ages just in case of an emergency, and this qualifies; it would certainly go a long way in helping him out. But conversely, we'll probably provoke an attack over some CDs and a bag of cash. It does make us sound like a bunch of criminals about to embark on a heist. But no, they're our CDs, and it's my cash. To hell with it! And them!

'We are united then?' Nephthys enquires.

And judging by all our expressions, we are. Was there ever really any doubt?

'You have all surpassed my expectations,' Nephthys continues. 'I am proud of what you have become, my children.'

As before, her physical form does tend to blur and unknit at times before weaving itself back together and — I think I mentioned the peculiar way she moves through the world earlier — it's as if the world turns to accommodate her new position and that she doesn't change her locus. It's easier to view this strange phenomenon from this outward perspective, but when, as earlier, we were walking with her, it felt like I was walking on one of those horizontal escalators you get at airports, but the wrong way. It felt very much like the world was turning beneath my feet. I just presumed, at the time, it was an after-effect of the bark, but it must be how Nephthys moves through this reality.

'You have risen to the many challenges that have been thrust upon you and dealt with them in a judicious and compassionate way. I could have asked for no more than what you have already achieved. You have elevated yourselves beyond what even the old gods consummated.'

Wow! Now that's a recommendation, something to add to my CV!

'But gods have merely been revered and worshipped by mortals primarily out of fear. Secretly harbouring jealous thoughts of attaining their powers and subverting their control. To take their very essence for themselves. It was inconceivable that we could live amongst them harmoniously. The veneration you all so deserve—'

I don't know about veneration — I'd just be happy if the military kept the hell off my property.

'—can only be achieved in your absence. Only then will you attest to their true worth. The random acts of kindness they are capable of, the love bestowed between family and friends. It is there, I have witnessed it for myself, felt it, but it is sadly marred by the darker nature of many of their kind. And despite all you have endured, you still wish to bestow this final gift upon them. My heart swells with pride.'

It's only an album! It is quite good, though. I think so anyway. If Deek does the business, you'll be able to judge for yourself soon. J did tell me once, though, that he believed music was the greatest gift humankind had been bestowed with, that it transcended new heights of consciousness, feeling and understanding, that it expunged barriers and breached the generation gap. Soothed troubled minds and aching hearts.

He's got that twinkle in his eye, and I break into a smile. I've been brooding again without realising it.

'But no unnecessary violence, okay? Unless we're provoked,' I reiterate.

'If they draw first blood, then we are obliged to respond in kind,' Ix concludes, having finally rejoined us and catching the end of the discussion after wrapping up her talk with Deek, who's trailing behind her in a bit of a stupor.

'You okay, Deek?'

He just nods. He's cool. He'll get over it. It takes a lot to make him speechless though.

'When do we depart?' Ix asks.

She's keen. I thought she would've been the one to be opposed to the idea.

'Yeah, we going now?'

Deek's found his voice again.

'I'm sorry, but I can't let you come along, Deek, not this time.' I can't justify his inclusion on this mission; the stakes are just too high. Besides, his presence could only endanger his future safety after the rest of us depart. If he's identified, they'll hunt him down, lock him up and throw away the key.

The disappointment on his face is apparent.

'Do not concern yourself, Deek, I will spill enough blood for the two of us.'

'Och, thanks, Mist, that means a lot.'

What? You think she was offering to drink a few beers on his behalf because he couldn't make it to a night out?

But Deek's savvier than he appears, and he realises what may befall him if he joins the assault, and he reluctantly hands over his assault rifle to Anastassia. Its presence in this place is strangely out of place and perhaps a little blasphemous.

She accepts the gift with a nod.

'So, is this goodbye then?'

'No, we will seek you out when we have the recordings.'

'Aye, I'm forgettin' about that, Mads.'

He nods in acceptance and grins, and I feel a little better, but before we knock some heads together, we should deliver Deek somewhere a little more Earthly, as I've images in my head of him leaping through dead people after we leave.

The portal I conjure manifests with an ease I have never encountered before as it appears as soon as I form the thought in my head.

'Your skills have sharpened,' Kal notes.

She's right. It's like when the eight of us were first reunited; I felt everything had been dialled up several notches. And now, with our full complement of nine in attendance — our ennead — I feel I could achieve almost anything.

'Transdimensional matter manipulation,' Nephthys more correctly ascribes, and she bestows me with a smile one would furnish a star pupil with.

'Shame you're not hangin' around, Nep, reckon you'd love *Stargate*.'

Nep! Is he serious? But she seems more bemused than insulted. Still, it was Deek that caused us all to call

Nyx, Nikki, and Medusa, Maddie. I just can't get with Mads, though — that's just something Deek calls her.

'Well, it sure beats takin' the bus,' Deek comments appreciatively as he steps through the transdimensional portal into my New York apartment, the safest place I can think of to deposit him.

'I'm sorry you're locked in for now. I left the keys in my other jeans.' I apologise, remembering locking the door after taking delivery of the takeaway and jamming the keys in my pocket.

'There is a spare set in the bedroom — you will find them in the hand.'

I give Maddie one of my looks at hearing this, eyebrow raised.

'The thing is about hands,' she says, 'is they tend to come in pairs.'

I dig J in the ribs as he tries to stifle a laugh — he's not helping.

'Are there any other body parts Deek should be made aware of?' I ask her.

She takes longer than I would have liked to respond.

'No.'

'You sure? You don't sound convinced.'

'Yes, I disposed of that other… ornament.'

Ornament! I don't want to know. 'Okay, Deek, do me a favour.'

'Sure, anything.'

162

'Throw that hand down the garbage chute when you get the opportunity.'

'Hand, garbage chute, check,' he confirms. 'Yous watch yourselves, okay?'

'We will return, rest assured.'

'Okey dokey, Ix.' He turns on the television and flings himself on the leather couch and calls up the digital guide with the remote. 'Oh, and thanks for the chat, by the way, Ix, appreciated.'

'It was my pleasure. It was knowledge you had earned.'

'But I've got one question afore yous go. Are ghosts real, then?'

You know what? It never occurred to me to ask about that.

'These are simply souls who have lost their way,' she answers.

'Och, that's what I thought.' And with his question answered to his satisfaction, he's already moved on and found something on one of the movie channels that has caught his attention. 'Braw, *Alien* is on in five.' And he settles down to watch it.

I shake my head. I'm going to say it. I'm flabbergasted at how Deek can just switch off and flip from being shown the mysteries of the afterlife to watching an old movie on the television in almost the same breath.

'Humans are resilient,' Nephthys comments as I draw the portal closed.

'I don't know if that's the word I would have used,' I reply.

'We should formulate a strategy before we embark,' Anastassia puts forward.

She's right, and I'm on it now that the decision has been made to go in. 'Ix, I'll leave it to you to bring us home.'

She nods.

'Far enough from the house so we can reconnoitre the area before moving in. If we can render any troops stationed in the vicinity unconscious, then we'll do so. As I said, I'd rather avoid conflict, but I also don't want to draw attention to ourselves as soon as we arrive. Let's keep the element of surprise for as long as we can. But if that doesn't work…'

'We know what to do.' Mist nods.

Nikki gives me a double thumbs up. It just doesn't look right when she does that; I'm going to have a quiet word with her.

I don't know why I'm worrying, considering the abilities we're packing. Essentially, I could open a portal and, between us all, take out the whole deployment of troops as fast as I can snap my fingers. But just in case I have a minor lapse of judgement or a stray bullet finds its mark… well, it's something I don't want to leave to chance. When the time comes, we're stepping through that portal together. I don't intend on attending a funeral before I leave.

A simple plan? What could possibly go wrong? Well, things very rarely pan out the way you foresee them happening.

16

Ix led us through an effortless transition, and everything was quiet upon our arrival — ominously so.

Due to the time difference with all the hopping about we'd done across time zones, it was dark here, which could prove to be advantageous to both sides or equally detrimental.

Maddie had removed her shades, and Anastassia had her rifle at hand as we spread out a little and slowly began to move forward.

This was it, the final showdown. A tumbleweed or two trundling past, wouldn't have been entirely out of context right now, or perhaps the theme tune from *A Fistful of Dollars*.

As we cautiously crept between shadows, our footfalls muffled by a simple charm I cast just to be safe, I was aware of the presence of intruders within the forest, and I looked for J for some confirmation. But his puzzled expression told me all I needed to know. As it turned out, the military had learnt since their last disastrous attempt at trying to capture us. This second deployment of troops had all been issued with headsets that emitted a low-frequency magnetic pulse that blocked J's attempts to accurately pinpoint their numbers and exact locations and prevented him from knocking them all out... again. Good for them, bad for us.

Looking back now, the fact that we neared my home, which was now just visible through the trees, without being accosted was all part of the plan. And it was at this precise moment when they launched their attack as a mix of flash-bang grenades and ones that issued a thick incapacitating gas rained down upon us from both flanks.

I automatically summoned a defensive shield as the first grenade detonated, but the effect of the flash-bangs had disorientated me, and my vision was lost for a few seconds, my ears ringing. But my senses were functioning well enough for me to make out the unmistakable sound of gunfire.

The magical defence wavered as I tried to take full control of my faculties again, my main objective to try to push back the spreading cloud of dense smoke that was threatening to engulf us.

I was completely disorientated, and the details of what I am about to relate to you were more firmly corroborated during the aftermath, as presently, the only members of my team I could distinguish in the confusion were J, Ix and Nephthys.

I noted Ix 'ghosting' as she immersed herself within the noxious gas and vanished from view as she pushed forward, the gas having no effect on her, at least in her current state.

Nephthys herself stepped into the cloud, passing straight through my shield, and summoned her powers, her hands stretching out before her, and the cloud of gas immediately began to unknit and disperse, like cold breath on a winter's morning.

At least that was one less problem to deal with, but what of the others? Together with J, I kept low as bullets continued to whizz past, tearing chunks out of the trees and kicking up sprays of dirt where they buried themselves in the ground.

I glimpsed Mist and Anastassia off on our left as the gas dispersed, each sheltering behind a tall pine tree, and as Anastassia returned fire from her position, a bullet clipped her arm, causing her to drop the rifle and clutch at the wound before drawing back into cover. This transpired at the same time as Kal took a hit from where she was, further ahead, attempting to close the gap between herself and the soldiers. I saw her body propelled back three times as she took three bullets to the shoulder and chest as the high-velocity rounds punched hard into her flesh. But she didn't fall. Two of her arms hung loosely down on one side, but she powered on, and just as my attention was distracted and my concentration wavered, J caught a bullet in the shoulder and was spun to the ground.

I immediately crouched down beside him and helped him reposition himself so he was propped up against a tree trunk out of the direct line of fire. He gave me a thumbs up and forced a smile, but I could see he was in a lot of pain, and there was a lot of blood seeping from between his fingers of the hand he had pressed over the wound.

This all happened in seconds, and my thoughts were scattered, but seeing J there, bleeding, my mind sharpened to a razor edge. I caught Mist's glacial eye where she was still taking shelter, and I gave her a nod — it was on. Despite our good intentions, all hope of negotiating some sort of peace was out of the window now. They'd invaded our home, already made a foolish attempt at capturing us before, and now they had shot my friends and my husband.

This was war, and it was one which I vowed they would sorely lose.

After our initial disorganisation, certainly on my part at least, events quickly spun in our favour as our ennead linked on a deeper level. We were as one from this point forward.

Yes, I had fully anticipated a far from friendly reception, but until we had been fired upon, there was a part of me that hadn't fully expected the violence we were dealt. And I think, no, I know, that the rest of the team were only awaiting my go-ahead before unleashing the full power we had at our beck and call. Well, most of them anyway.

And what must Nephthys be thinking? This is some welcome committee to be faced with, her first real physical encounter with the outside world in centuries.

The gas cloud was fully diffused now, and Nephthys appeared beside me to examine J's wound. I had noticed as she casually walked over, as if taking a relaxing stroll, that several bullets found their mark as she presented an easy target, but they simply passed through her, her physical body unknitting where the projectiles struck her and weaving together again after they exited her body.

'Let me see.'

J complied and removed his hand; I couldn't help but gasp and cover my mouth. That was a lot of blood.

Nephthys then held two fingers above the hole, and I watched on in fascination as the skin was woven back together, an identical miracle performed on the exit wound and presumably all the muscle in between. Not even scar tissue remained to mark the injury.

'Thanks.' J rolled his shoulder, testing it. 'Good as new,' he confirmed, but he was still white as a sheet as a result of blood loss and shock.

As this healing was taking place, Mist had broken cover and had spun her axe end over end until it found its target, burying itself deep into one of the soldiers, splitting his facemask and the flesh and bone beneath it. Anastassia cut down another with a spray of bullets after retrieving the fallen rifle. As Mist strode purposefully forward to retrieve her axe, she made a casual, dismissive gesture with her right hand, and I noted four soldiers toppling from behind their respective trees, dead before they hit the ground. This was the first time

I had truly witnessed her Valkyrian powers on the battlefield. Another two quickly fell before her wrath, and I can empathise with how she must have felt after Anastassia took a hit, but the consummate trooper she is, she was still very much in the game.

With J now restored, together with Nephthys, we regroup with Mist and Anastassia. My focus is absolute now and spotting a soldier making a hasty retreat, I conjure a portal before his fleeing form, catching him unawares, and he stumbles through before he can catch himself. I see a vista of white beyond before I seal it, a flurry of snow filling the air for a moment before quickly settling and melting into the ground. I hope he was wearing his thermals.

Mist has levered her axe free from the soldier's face, the noise, I have to admit, made me cringe. Although I am a horror movie aficionado and the sight of visceral horror on-screen doesn't leave me feeling squeamish, the very real sight and sound of someone having an axe removed from their face is an altogether different matter.

We sense movement and turn as one to face the threat as a further two soldiers in proximity have decided that retreat is their best option right now but before I can react, or Mist, J catches one with a massive telekinetic surge and sends him flying, and he slams face-first into a tree trunk and tumbles to the ground. That had to hurt. I think J was seeking some retribution for being shot.

Nephthys deals with the other. All she does is tilt her head, and he begins to unravel. That's how it appears at this distance, at least, and before he's covered ten yards, he's gone — not even a uniform is left in his wake.

Kal soon joins our ranks, her black cotton shirt hiding the full extent of her wounds, but I can see the fabric plastered to her body, and her two upper left arms are slick with blood. The two swords she would normally wield with those arms are sheathed, but the remaining four are painted bright red.

Nephthys immediately steps up and performs her healing magic, the wounds closing together after the bullets are drawn out from where they lie embedded deep in the muscle. A very handy team member to have in the field. I would have never had the skill to perform such surgery. Maybe I could, on reconsideration, but like Maddie, I merely lacked the confidence.

Once she has fixed up Kal, she seals the graze in Anastassia's upper arm, little more than a deep cut.

Speaking of Maddie, she and the others had ploughed into the troops stationed on both our flanks as soon as the gunfire had commenced, clearing the immediate area before pressing their advantage and advancing on the troops stationed in and around our studio and home, as we were informed by Sophia who was the next member of our team to show up.

Her golden fire lit up the forest as she floated through the trees and dropped a soldier in our midst from a sufficient height to break a leg. Anastassia was quick to grab the luckless woman, on this occasion, and pin her against a tree by the throat with her prosthetic arm.

Sophia then floated back down to Earth, her sword firmly clutched in one hand. Incidentally, I noticed later on, that bullets simply disappear in a flare of fiery light as soon as they enter her aura.

Shooting at an angel — sorry, Seraphim — can you believe the audacity of that?

'I brought you a present. I thought we could question her.'

Good thinking, but I'm not sure Mist is big on interrogation as she places the blade of her axe against our captive's forehead after first ripping off her facemask. This is when we first noticed the magnetic pulse device.

'This was blocking my psychic abilities,' J concludes, briefly examining the headset before discarding it. 'How many more of you are there in the house?'

The soldier just continues to struggle against Anastassia's unbreakable hold.

'I would answer if I were you, or I will allow my wife to slice off the top of your skull, and then we will return your head to your family so they can use it as a cookie jar.'

That got her vocal cords working.

'Forty troops in total, about a dozen in the house,' she manages to wheeze out through partially crushed vocal cords. 'Are you going to kill me?'

I notice Anastassia glance at her bloodied sleeve where the bullet grazed her and Kal's blood-soaked top before answering. 'Yes.' And with a slight pressure, she crushed her throat and let her body slide to the ground.

With Sophia's assurance that all the active troops are indeed holed up further ahead, we begin to advance. We can still hear the unmistakable thump of grenades going off and witness plumes of dirt erupting into the air as the embedded soldiers attempt to repel Maddie and Nikki.

Ix flits — like the ghost she is at present — from soldier to soldier as she approaches the house, and they fall at her touch, rendered immediately unconscious. Though I witness her pass straight through the body of one soldier and momentarily consider what that must have felt like as he drops.

Please don't judge us too harshly, reader. Despite all that I am sharing with you, none of us are cold-blooded killers. And the thought of taking another's life is repellent to me. But I have to admit, at the time this was playing out, I felt no pity or remorse. Even when I sent that soldier through a portal, and I would only be fooling myself if I was to say that they were still alive, I can't. I just thought of somewhere cold and remote to send them. And if someone were to ask me off the top of my head to think of somewhere cold and remote, I'd think Antarctica. So, unless an exploration party picked them up, then they have undoubtedly been ice-cubed.

Ix is also very much an advocate for life, and I'm convinced that those soldiers who felt her touch will at some point regain consciousness. I wish I could say the same for those unfortunates who encountered Maddie and Nikki.

As we skirted the periphery of the forest furthest from the house before then making for the studio, we noticed the first of Maddie's 'statues'. Most were lying prone in the dirt in peculiar positions of retreat — even clothes and weaponry had been solidified. This was an aspect I hadn't been aware of before. Maybe she had always been capable of this. Or perhaps it was a result of her newfound liberty.

The area surrounding my property looked like an army car park on the moon — there were so many craters due to the numerous grenades. I could identify three Humvees, two APCs — Armoured Personnel Carriers — and at least two Jeeps, one of which was upside down, everything from the chassis up completely crushed. And I just knew there was a body under there, one which Nikki had flattened with complete precision. And that was just the backyard.

The ground in between the vehicles and craters was littered with bodies, calcified or otherwise. Nikki's victims were far less tidy, so to speak, as the ground was scattered with several particularly gory body parts where she had simply ripped her targets apart. The door to the studio was lying open. Muffled gunfire could be heard from inside, and a grenade went off before a soldier rushed out of the building with Nikki in close pursuit, phasing into her shadow form just as she caught up with him, and similarly, as I had witnessed Ix perform, she passed straight through him. Although I'm quite sure the experience was entirely different as the soldier spasmed as if a high voltage charge had been put through his body, and he skidded to a halt face down on the hard-packed dirt.

A couple of grenades sailed into view as we hurried to regroup with Nikki, but the umbrella shield I deployed dispersed the explosion above our heads. The result from our perspective was quite spectacular.

'Where's Maddie?' I asked as soon as we regrouped and, as one, retreated into the studio. The solid construction should at least protect us for now from further assault, but the interior was chaotic. The wood was riddled with bullet holes, and the grenade we had heard had ripped a massive gouge out of one of the interior walls and shattered the glass panel that separated the recording booth from the rest of the studio. The floor was strewn with papers and broken soldiers.

'Here,' she called out, much to my relief. 'I was retrieving something for Anastassia,' she explained before appearing from the lounge clutching a rifle, a stone hand still in place, the stone finger curled around the trigger. She snapped off the appendage before handing it to her.

'Thank you. This one is empty.' Anastassia discarded the one she still carried and checked the breach and magazine of the new one, nodding in satisfaction at what she found.

'You are injured?' Maddie asked in genuine concern as she noted the torn, blood-soaked garments.

'It looks worse than it is,' Kal allayed her concern. 'Nephthys healed our wounds.' She dipped her head in thanks.

'These mortals have murder in mind,' Nephthys states simply.

J nods. 'Yeah, I picked that up loud and clear from the one Sophia flew in.'

Nikki flicks him a curious look.

'The soldier is dead,' Anastassia answers. 'We are not here to take hostages.'

Nikki smiles, and I note her teeth and mouth are thick with blood — a smile that would chill a great white, I think — apparently, she has been utilising more than just her shadow form and natural strength to neutralise the threat.

'Do not worry, Alice.' She spots my look. 'I did not partake. In fact, I found the taste explicitly repellent,' she confesses. 'But needs must, in times such as these.'

'Yes,' Maddie agrees. 'But you may find you now possess a small stone army to accompany your bear.'

'I noticed. But it is no more than they deserve.'

Maddie smiles at me. This is probably the only time I haven't admonished her for using her power on people.

Although I had no qualms with her helping dispose of Nikki's leftovers in the past. But this is the first time any of us have used our abilities in such a way. Perhaps if we had decided to don spangly outfits, the military might have been more willing to accept us — I doubt it, though. But if someone attacks you… well, you defend yourself, and if that someone attempts to take your life, well…

'I have the recordings,' Mist informs us holding up a clutch of CDs after rummaging around amongst the debris in the recording room.

At least they weren't trashed in the carnage.

'And according to the information we retrieved, there are probably only about a dozen troops left in the house,' J confirms. 'But unless we act fast, that number is going to seriously increase, and the next time, they'll be using heavier artillery.'

J was right. Perhaps up until now, their overconfidence and sheer arrogance had led to their missions failing. Relying, as they always do, on their guns and training. But I doubt whether we'd come out victorious if they hit us with a few missiles.

'I will survey the area,' Sophia volunteered and glided from the studio.

We waited for a short while as she scouted ahead, the sound of gunfire filling the air once more as she revealed herself.

'This place is completely trashed,' Anastassia commented as she glanced around.

'My guitar is broken,' Mist revealed through clenched teeth.

Oh shit! If you thought she was mad before…

'It is riddled with bullet holes.'

I did wonder why she wasn't looking more pleased when she returned from the recording room with the CDs.

'I would present you with the perpetrator to exact your punishment for such a defilement, but I tore his throat out,' Nikki answers.

'That is satisfactory,' Mist grunts, still rather pissed off.

'Where's Ix?' I suddenly realised the last I saw of her was when she was approaching the house.

'Do not worry. Our emissary of death has transitioned; no harm will avail her. She clears your home of infiltrators; she will complete her task soon.'

Emissary of death? Not sure if Ix will be over the moon with Nephthys' turn of phrase. Then again, I suppose, in a way, that is exactly what she is!

Sophia breezes back in like a warm summer breeze. I realise that's rather out of context considering the amount of blood and stone body parts we're standing amongst, but that's how she entered!

She shakes her head and sighs. 'The house is clear. Ix has the one in command in her thrall. Three eluded me and are sealed within one of the vehicles, and I am ashamed to admit that I had to deal with two others. There is also a sniper located in the trees off to the left of the house, but…' She sighs again. 'I tire of all this death.'

I'm quite sure that despite Sophia having 'dealt' with two soldiers that she refrained from killing them — it's just not in her nature.

'He's mine.' Maddie calls dibs on the sniper.

'Do you think so?' Nikki raises an eyebrow.

'No,' Kal firmly insinuates herself. 'I still have a score to settle.'

Nobody argues.

'What about the three in the truck?'

'Mine,' J determinedly volunteers. 'Give me a second, Kal, and I'll take care of them before you go.'

J reaches back for my hand, and I grab it, interlacing my fingers with his, and he pulls me over to the window, what's left of it anyway, and peers through the shattered pane.

What happened next took place in literally two or three seconds.

As soon as we were spotted looking out, the fifty-calibre gun that was installed on the APC in question thudded into life. I put up a shield, and the heavy rounds flattened against its invisible surface and fell to the ground whilst J compressed that armoured vehicle to about the size of a Mini. There were still flattened rounds dropping to the dirt like coins after the armoured plated truck had been crushed; it happened that fast.

Kal claps J on the shoulder. 'Nice work.' She strolls out of the cabin.

'Impressive telekinetic projection skills,' Nephthys commends, but the comment is tinged with sadness. 'If only there had been an alternative course of action with which to resolve this dilemma.'

J nods in agreement, also taking little pleasure from his bittersweet victory.

I feel much the same as them, and already I'm beginning to wonder if this has all been worth it.

I quickly release J and jog after Kal, noting as I exit the recording studio that Yogi has taken a few direct hits and now resembles a rough boulder with three legs. I quickly catch her up. Despite my feelings, I'm not letting my friend catch another bullet, and I arrive just in time to deflect a well-aimed sniper round, that whistles past us. This time I just know when and where to project a hasty charm, and the bullet goes wild. Kal nods in thanks as I try something different. This time the bullet transforms into a delicate pink blossom and caresses Kal's cheek gently, and flutters to the carpet of pine needles underfoot.

I shrug. 'I couldn't help myself.'

Kal laughs. 'Very impressive, enchantress.'

A third bullet is similarly transformed; this time I barely have to exert any effort at all. And now Kal has located the sniper's whereabouts; she then proves to me that she is just as adept at throwing swords as Mist is at throwing her axe. The scimitar she selected for the task cleaving the shooter's head.

'Now that was impressive,' I commend.

'The scimitar's weight is perfectly balanced for throwing,' she explains.

I wait until she retrieves her sword, I don't need to witness close hand another gory extraction again, and together we make for the house where the rest of the team have regathered, including Ix, who has the tips of the fingers of one ghosted hand inserted into the commander's skull. I wasn't even aware she could ghost parts of her body separately. All these personal developments have to be a result of our ennead being fully restored.

Before I relate this final scene to you, you may be wondering that with having access to all these incredible and powerful gifts, why didn't we — for instance — send Nephthys in, or anyone for that matter, to wipe out all resistance? Good point, and yes, any one of the ennead could have done so, I'm quite sure. But it's one thing fighting demons and monsters, it's quite another battling with human beings, however misguided and stupid they are. And, personally at least, although I'm not the only one, I had still harboured some sliver of hope that at some point they would have thrown down their weapons and surrendered. How foolish I was. You can only learn from your mistakes, after all.

'Well, Commander, it's just us now.' I approach the seated officer, and Ix retrieves her hand with evident relief on her face.

His shifty eyes settle on me as I confront him, and his lip pulls back in a sneer below an impressive moustache — if it was the 1970s!

'His mind is a cesspit,' Ix warns me, grimacing, her hand solidifying as she steps aside.

'You okay?'

'Yes, but we would do well to vacate this place soon,' she advises.

I notice the presence of several bodies lying strewn about the room and sprawled on the stairs, evidence of Ix's work, before turning my attention to the man in charge seated before me. 'Why, Commander?' I've got to know.

'It's Major, actually.' The middle-aged uniform sneers at me with contempt. 'Because you are a threat to our national security.'

'A threat? Are you serious?' I'm shocked by the insinuation.

And I'm not the only one who clocks the glance he casts at his holstered sidearm. Kal takes up a position directly behind him, where he's seated, and firmly grips his neck with a blue hand.

'One move,' she advises. Her intentions are quite clear.

I'm sorely tempted to punch him in the face as I cast a weary gaze over the once pristine interior of the home I once cherished. Boot prints, muddy and melted ice-creamy trail tracks across the hardwood floor. Radio equipment is set up on my tea table next to a vinyl disc that has been used as a coaster! I'm really struggling not to hit him now.

'Shit, now you've done it, Major,' J says as he spots the defiled disc.

I hear Maddie tutting in the background; she knows the score.

And don't even get me started on the rest of the mugs and dishes that festoon the living room. And, bastards! I've just caught a glimpse of the label on that disc — it's one of my Bowie first presses!

If I could blow steam out of my ears right now — cartoon-style — I would.

I'll give him his dues, this major, despite being surrounded by our full team, his own now either wiped out, unconscious or freezing his or her arse off in Antarctica, is keeping his cool.

'You may have won this battle, but the war is far from over.'

How woefully predictable, boring and clichéd. He could have put a bit more effort in than that. A reflection of his low intellect, no doubt.

'You'll be hunted down every last one of you. There won't be a place anywhere on this planet you'll be able to hide.'

'Perhaps not in this dimension,' Nephthys responds with a twitch of a smile.

'And who the fuck are you? Another freak signed up to your band of misfits?'

'Without Nephthys' aid, you would still be faced with a full-blown invasion,' I remind him. Ungrateful git!

'I have only your word for that. One which I am not inclined to believe.'

'And where's the other one?' The major tries to turn his head, but Kal's grip is solid. 'Loitering outside?'

'We let him go,' Nikki informs him. 'His own opinions and objectives clashed with our own.'

'At least one of you saw sense,' he huffs.

Good one, Nikki. That may have lifted some of the heat off Deek.

'What shall we do with you, Major?' Nikki strokes her chin as she contemplates his fate.

He's sweating profusely now — and so he should — I've got some decidedly unpleasant alternatives running through my head right now.

'You and these freaks' — he almost spat the word — 'have just assaulted the US Marines. I'll see you in chains for this.'

So, that's who they were. They considered the so-called threat we presented sufficient to call in the Marines.

'Idle threats, Major,' Ix informs him.

Mist's in his face now. 'I have been held in chains before; no one will ever do such to me again. I will rip your spine out and strangle you with it first!'

Calm down! I've got visions of this turning into a scene from *Hostel*.

She's holding up her bloodied axe so he can have a good look. 'After I have peeled off your skin first.'

'And that' — the major points out Anastassia's arm, completely ignoring Mist's threat — 'is the property of the United States Army.'

Anastassia delivers him a swift rabbit punch to the face that bloodies his nose and dyes his moustache a bright crimson.

I didn't see that coming.

'It belongs to me.'

'Hah!' Maddie enjoyed that.

'What are you going to do to me?'

You know what? I think the major is beginning to worry now about his continued existence.

'I could unravel you, strand by strand, thread by thread,' Nephthys suggests. 'It would be as if you never even existed.' She raises a perfectly shaped black eyebrow as if awaiting his permission to begin.

'What do you think, Major? You fancy that?'

Then, he actually spits on me — the pig! How gross!

J delivers him an impressive right hook that splits his lip and possibly loosened a few teeth as well. 'That's my wife.'

I shake my head at Kal as I see the major's face start to turn purple, and she relaxes her hold.

'It is time we finished this and were gone.' Sophia speaks up and lowers her ethereal flaming sword so the tip rests a millimetre in front of the major's nose before lowering it, and with extreme precision, she hooks a gold chain that hangs around his neck and lifts it free of his Kevlar vest to reveal the crucifix that dangles there. 'There is no God, Major, only us.' Her voice drops in cadence as she delivers her certitude.

That gave me goosebumps, but she's right, we should be skedaddling — I like that word — we don't use it enough these days, along with vamoose. An idea had just occurred to me, and I began to navigate the debris littering the floor and the bodies on the stairs. Okay, I didn't step over the two strewn on the stairs; I stepped on them. Okay, I admit it. I stomped on them a bit. I was still pissed about my vinyl. I know it's only stuff… but still, it was my stuff.

'Don't kill him,' I shout over my shoulder.

'Would I?' Nikki answers.

'Yes,' I shout back.

My anger has subsided a bit after my stomping, and I'm reluctant to slaughter this twonk — yay, I finally got to use that word!

I try to ignore the fact when I enter my bedroom that someone's been sleeping in my bed. And it wasn't bloody Goldilocks! I don't even want to know what state my bathroom's in! I hurry over to my walk-in wardrobe and, much to my relief, the holdall of cash is still where I had it buried under a luggage set. I then

187

reach up an arm and feel along the top shelf, rummaging between shoe boxes until my fingers close on what I've been hunting for. Then before returning downstairs, I rip off my soiled top and sling it to the floor — what the hell! — and pull on a clean sweater. I then bound back down the stairs and, without explanation, I throw Nikki the bag of money and dash into the kitchen and begin rummaging frantically through kitchen drawers until I find the tube of superglue still in its packaging.

J raises an eyebrow when I return, barely suppressing a smile.

We're all adults here, aren't we? And in my defence, before J, it got lonely out here in the wilderness sometimes before the Pariahs took residence. Still, I can feel myself blushing.

'What?'

'I never said a word,' Sophia replies, but she's smirking; she likes where this is going.

I also note the major's eyebrows almost leaving his face as he sees the sex toy I'm holding for the first time, and I'm struggling not to fall into hysterics.

After removing the tube of glue from the packaging, I realise I don't have anything to pierce the applicator with. 'Kal?'

She obliges and nips off the end with one of her bloodied katanas.

I then empty the tube on his head — yes, his head, what were you thinking? — before erecting the sex toy in place and holding it there until it is firmly bonded.

His bald head is perfect for the operation, and it stands proud when I'm done.

'Hah!' Maddie barks her approval.

'*Zalupa*!' Anastassia exclaims before giving in to hysterics.

I think that's Russian for dick-head.

Even Nephthys covers her mouth and averts her gaze as she struggles to contain her laughter.

'I like your style.' J catches me in a hug and plants a kiss on my cheek.

Now everyone's struggling to maintain their composure. It's funny that when faced with something or someone deplorable or threatening, the most effective way to defuse the situation is to laugh at it.

Sophia's body is wracked with laughter as she steps forward and bats the appendage with her hand, and it wobbles in response.

'Well, Major' — I'm really struggling to keep it together now — 'we'll be off.'

'But before we do' — Nikki leans in and plants a kiss on his forehead before slapping his cheek playfully — 'enjoy your nightmares.'

'You can do that?' J asks in surprise as she strides past him.

'Goddess of night... dreams and nightmares.'

Now that the major realises that we are going to spare him, we are assailed by a stream of expletives as we make to leave, but I don't care, I'm still laughing.

I turn around as I hear Nephthys tutting. The major has stood up now that Kal has relinquished her hold, and he has unholstered his sidearm, which, much to his disbelief, is unravelling before his very eyes.

'You foolish mortal,' she admonishes as she walks past, shaking her head, the beads in her braided hair tapping together lightly.

'Firing blanks, Major?' Nikki calls back.

Sophia can barely walk upright with laughing now, and she rockets into the air as soon as she exits the house like a firework.

Mist takes possession of the holdall and places the CDs inside before also leaving. Maddie nips back, looks the major in the eye and, for a second, I thought she was going to ossify him.

'Look into my eye, Major.'

He can hardly not, and with that, Maddie scoots through the door with a smile. She just can't see Nikki getting in the last blow. Seconds later, from where we are all now gathered outside, I hear the major roaring.

'What did you do, Maddie?' I've got to know. 'You didn't?' I'm convinced that sex toy has just sparked her imagination.

'No, but only because I didn't think of it,' she admits. 'I turned his trigger finger to stone. And, no, that was not a euphemism.'

Our mission was complete, and now when I look back, I can't help but smile when I picture the major. I'm glad it ended like that, at least. That home has provided us with a lot of happy memories, and I didn't want that memory tainted by the battle that took place there. I should have delivered the major to A&E before we left and given the staff on duty a good laugh — never mind.

From there, I conveyed us directly to New York, where Deek was glued to the television, watching Ripley being hunted down by the alien.

He turned around as we fully arrived, the portal closing behind us. 'You didnae bring anything to eat, did yous? I'm starved. There's nothing in, and I didnae have any cash on me to order a takeaway.'

17

Now that we had foiled the major and his dastardly plan, our time was drawing to a close, but we had time to spare now, and Deek listened in rapt attention as we relived the encounter. He even neglected the climax of the movie and exploded into fits of laughter, slapping the armrest of the couch in appreciation as I told him about the major's new prosthetic.

'Och, you shoulda taken a photo. That would've definitely been posted online.'

Not a bad idea, but we'd all fallen out of the habit of carrying mobiles — some of the team had never really taken to the habit anyway, realising how easily they can be tracked. But thanks to Nikki's quick thinking, Deek had been firmly placed out of events, which would hopefully see him safe in the future.

Once our escapades had been shared, I handed him the bag. 'For you.'

After unzipping it and peering in, he quickly zipped it up again and stared at me with big, round eyes.

'About half a million,' I explain. 'Canadian dollars and pound sterling, though, I'm afraid. Didn't have time to change it.'

'Thanks, Alice. All of you. But you didnae need to do this, ye ken?'

'Yes, I ken.'

'The discs are in the bag also,' Mist reminds him.

'No need to worry about that; I'll get that sorted out — you can count on me.' He grins back and takes another peek inside the bag. 'Holy—'

'Shit!' I finish for him.

'Will you manage by yourself?' Maddie asks, genuinely concerned about his future well-being.

'Mads, I'll be fine, dinnae yous worry. I've got ma passport.' He taps his pocket. 'An' a bag o' cash. What more could I want?'

'And this place for as long as you want it as well,' I add. 'The deeds are under a false name, and all the bills are paid through an untraceable account, so you'll be safe enough.'

He stands up and folds me in a hug before sitting back down to take us all in.

J claps him on the shoulder. 'You all right, mate?'

'Och.' He wipes at his eyes. 'You guys are the best.'

Shit, I'm getting misty-eyed now as well! A part of me still wishes he was coming along, though. I'm going to miss his Scottish wit and attitude to life, even if some of his banter is still incomprehensible to me, especially when he's — as he puts it, 'when I'm pished'. But I fully understand that he's still got a full life ahead of him, whereas we've all lived so many, ones that we can readily remember, and as a consequence of that, we're very much ready for the next step. Angry military types chasing us around the globe aside. And our crossing over was how I had envisioned it all that time ago, together as one family, the Pariahs.

But there was still something we were curious about, and I encourage Deek to flip the channel.

Now perhaps you — if you're still with me? Yes, there you are — see events a little differently. A behind-the-curtains peek, so to speak. But for those who remain oblivious to our involvement, the Nephilim invasion may come across as rather drab and disappointing. They materialised in our midst, filled with impending doom, then, sometime later, they fell over. Not the kind of event 20th Century Fox is going to make a billion-dollar blockbuster about. But who said all victories should come at the price of global warfare? Besides, wait until the authorities see what we left them back in Canada!

There were minor casualties, of course, such as those we witnessed online courtesy of Maddie, but the toppling of the defeated giants did inevitably rack up the body count a little, as some people weren't quick enough on their feet. Including one individual who was filmed haranguing the crowd about the evils of warfare — obviously, he must have thought these Nephilim were military prototypes — and was so preoccupied with his rant he was nailed into the ground. Maddie, in particular, enjoyed that one immensely.

Other instances involved crushed buildings, vehicles and a few people with guns. Even a Marmite factory! No, I'm only kidding, but I was crossing my fingers. But generally, as we flipped channels to gain different perspectives, it was pretty much the same worldwide.

'They are about to retrieve the one in the park,' Ix informs us from where she's standing, her face reflected eerily back into the room off the glass of the window, the scenes depicted on the television holding little interest for her.

We joined her, our curiosity getting the better of us. It was close to dawn now, and the sky was beginning to fade to a cobalt blue. But we could clearly make out the crimson Nephilim. This one had remained upright, picked out by the array of portable spotlights that now surrounded her, lighting her up. And in the street below, an open bed truck was being waved through the crowd that the military was holding in check whilst the truck driver — military, of course — backed the vehicle towards an access road that meandered through the park. It had begun. More alien tech for the boffins to play with, and who knew what this could spell for the future of the human race. Action figures, I would imagine.

I'll omit our final farewells with Deek as it will only upset me again, but we sat with him for a while reminiscing until dawn had broken, and I caught him yawning.

'Boring you?'

'No, Nep, no, I'm just dead beat.'

Nep! Again! What's he like? I could tell she was joking — that was an aspect of humanity she rapidly caught onto. But it was indeed time to leave. Departing was not going to become any easier the longer we delayed.

18

We're standing on the brink of something quite momentous right now, gathered before the portal in that place in between. Anastassia marvelling once more at the return of her flesh arm. I guess that is a miracle all who have suffered an amputation in their lives will experience in this place before moving on whole once more.

We are all similarly imbued with excitement and expectation, and I couldn't comprehend earlier what exactly I would be feeling when finally faced with taking that final step. But it's all good, even knowing that once it's done, there is no going back. It's a small death in a way, it comes to us all, and the Pariahs and I are very fortunate to have been granted this opportunity. But boy, did it come with a price.

Sophia is brimming over with exuberance, streamers of golden light spiralling around her. I think some of the newly deceased, those more sensitive than others, have caught something of her out of the corner of their eye as I've noticed one or two glancing over. But Sophia, being a divine being herself, in many ways was the least suited to an extended stay on the Earth plane, and she is eager to be moving onwards.

Just before I scoot off, I must thank you for your constant companionship throughout everything that has transpired. It quite literally — or is that literary? — wouldn't have been the same without you.

I'll leave you with a final profound thought that occurred to me regarding an all-powerful God or deity or however you perceive such things if you are religiously inclined. That image now seems to me to have been more of a prophetic vision of what could be — or was — let's just say the position has now been filled. That's the conclusion I came to after a short conversation with Nephthys; all these ancient gods had been vying for the sole claim of chairman of the board, so to speak, and we nipped in and pipped them to the post. Although by the time we'd finished there was no competition left! In that sense, then, we aren't entirely abandoning you, and if you pray really hard, maybe Maddie will hear you and turn your boss to stone... no, that won't happen, but you know what I'm getting at. Or perhaps you need a demon slaying? I'm sure we could accommodate that.

We're going now, the others have passed over, and J's taken his first step, and he's pulling me by the hand. So, be good because you never know who may be watching...

EPILOGUE

You didn't think I'd leave things like that, did you? I'm sure you've still got some burning questions you'd like answered, like, if you crossed into this divine, magical realm, then how come I'm reading this book right now, narrated by me? How's Deek faring by himself? Was J Merlin in a past life? Is Santa Claus real? And who's my favourite Harry Potter character?

Firstly, I'll deal with the three latter questions... in order. No, Merlin, as it turns out, is indeed a fictitious character, I'm not telling and Hermione, of course.

Now to the matter of this novel you're clutching in your hands, thinking, *Get on with it!* Since our time in this place, we Pariahs have been bestowed with great gifts and, of course, responsibilities. Gifts, I hasten to add, that make our previous abilities pale somewhat in comparison. And as a consequence, we are capable of intervening and influencing events on Earth, all for the greater good, I hasten to add. Minor miracles you may have noticed, for instance, well, that was probably down to us. But we've still got a bit of work to do as the place is a bit of a mess, to put it bluntly. The previous elder gods threw one last hurrah before being vanquished, so we'll be sweeping up streamers, picking up partially deflated balloons and empty beer cans for a while yet, in a manner of speaking, that is. Plastic everywhere and innumerable unsavoury types inhabiting the world, but we're working on it; you'll just have to be patient and lend a hand, of course, when you can from time to time.

Now, the book you're reading, although narrated by me, is largely thanks to J and his telepathic powers. All our gifts have grown exponentially since we crossed — Nephthys pulled the stops out when she wove this place, by the way — so if you've woken one morning having had a wonderful dream or perhaps conversely from a sweat-sheathed nightmare, you'll have Nikki to thank, or curse, for that. Or maybe you've had a divine epiphany. That would be thanks to Sophia. Or maybe your little dog isn't looking too lively today and resembles more of a statue — Maddie. I'm just joking regarding that one.

It's a shame in a way that you didn't get the opportunity to get to know Nephthys better, but if you experience a magical moment, well…

Anyway, it was simplicity itself for J to psychically make contact with a budding author and transcribe my narrative via telepathic communication. See, pretty straightforward, really.

While I'm on the subject of J, I'll refer now to some of his past lives, which I'm sure you're eager to learn about, as was I. Like my own experience, numerous nameless faces flashed across his mind fleetingly, many of which would mean little to you like Christopher

Hempworth, a psychic medium who lived during the Victorian era, gifted but not very well renowned. Ever heard of him? Neither had I. Some of his more noteworthy personas were: Dōgen Zenji, a Japanese Buddhist priest from the thirteenth century and the Count of Saint Germain. A count no less! Who claimed to have lived, for over five hundred years. Yeah, and the rest! A great philosopher, amongst other things, and a bit of a 'lad' by eighteenth-century standards. He did mention Grigori Rasputin as well, you know, the mad monk. But I'm sure he was having me on with regards to that one. No, he's shaking his head; he assures me that is one of the lives he picked up on. And he wasn't mad, he was a mystic. Okay, sorry.

Then also worth mentioning is Edward Kelley, who claimed that he communicated with angels. Which got me wondering whether this previous incarnation of J's was somehow telepathically in touch with our very own Sophia. Perhaps her divinity granted her that access? Or maybe God himself allowed it? It's plausible, but... J's shrugging — he doesn't know. It was a very long time ago, after all. But it does get you thinking, or at least it got me thinking, as to whether there had been further subverted contact passing between us over the centuries, keeping in touch, keeping our dream alive and further undermining those deities who still claimed power over us.

So, between us, we have accumulated quite a historical pedigree and amassed an impressive knowledge of eras past.

Deek, yes, he's doing very well. As you've probably gathered or even heard, he did manage to successfully put our third album out there. And yes, the military did eventually track him down, but he played it cool and dumb, and he was released shortly after as he had nothing of interest to divulge. His lack of 'powers' meant that they had little interest in him anyway; it was us that they were specifically after. Good luck with that! He's currently living it up in Brazil at the moment with a rather pretty local woman — good for him. I don't know how she's coping with his accent, though.

Ah, some things never change. I can hear guitar chords wafting through the aether. Well, why give up what you love, right? We still play for our enjoyment, and it allows us to relax and recharge; it's hard work sorting the planet out. And in our world, 'Stairway to Heaven' is no longer denied! Do you get that one? *Wayne's World*? No? I don't know why I bother. Deek would have got that one. It's one of many classic tunes we like to play as well as writing new material. Some of which we may well bestow upon talented musicians — a little divine inspiration to help progress their careers. So, if you catch a good tune online or on the radio — do people still listen to that? — it may well have its origins in an otherworldly realm.

It's time I properly signed off and released J from his deep focus. It takes a lot of concentration to relate the entirety of a novel to a mortal soul — he's a star. He smiled at me just then and gave me a thumbs up.

So, farewell, my faithful reader. I can see you there curled up on your couch nibbling on some chocolate, and you, cosied up in bed, and you catching some rays on the beach whilst enjoying a well-earned holiday. Stay good, or you may just wake up in the dead of night to discover a floating skull-face haunting the shadows of your bedroom!

Ix is shaking her head in denial; she wouldn't do that to you. I know, I was joking. Am I the only one around here with a sense of humour?

You've spoilt my ending now!

PARIAHS
III

Axe Attack
Live for the Night
Face of an Angel
Bad Times... Good Friends
Take My Hand
You Know What I'm Thinking
Out of the Blue
Demon Slayer
Immortality
Heaven Sent
Love Punch

Bonus Tracks:
(Don't Fear) The Reaper (Live at The Forum, California)
Looks That Kill (Live at Glastonbury)

CODA

It was whilst we were on the road to our next venue — Athens, if you're interested — that my attention was caught by an unusual report about an event that occurred in the Kampong Thom province of Cambodia. A team of scientists had been reported missing whilst studying the natural biology of the area in question. Naturally, a search party had then been quickly appointed and deployed.

Now, since our encounter with that deranged underworld goddess and her monstrous contrivances, I had fallen into the habit of frequently checking certain websites that specialised in unexplained mysteries and sightings of strange creatures. Much of which turned out to be fictionalised nonsense. But I still harboured the suspicion that some of Her creations had perhaps escaped everyone's attention and still roamed some of the remoter parts of the world.

J also fell into this habit of surfing the net with me in search of creature sightings, his interest in cryptozoology lending itself well to this vigilance, and he directed me to the best sites to regularly check.

Travelling between gigs can be rather tedious at times, especially as now it was Sophia's choice of DVD entertainment — *The Greatest Showman* — and much grumbling ensued from the others at her selection. I've got to admit I quite like it. But it was her turn, and to be honest, it made a change from the *Avengers*. So, she and Ix are firmly glued to the screen. Ix is so accommodating anyway. Kal and Nikki played chess. This is something I can play, but together with J, they're really good, and I got quickly tired of being hammered every time I was challenged. And I refuse to play Scrabble with Nikki again as she uses such archaic words all the time, ones that I've never come across in any dictionary I've ever referred to!

Mist and Anastassia are practising, headphones plugged in so the rest of us can gain a little peace, and Maddie is keeping Deek company as he drives the bus, relating to her one of his many escapades.

So, J and I have managed to secure the onboard laptop for a while and are touring the regular sites — that's when we struck gold, so to speak.

The disappearance of six experts in their fields of biology, geology and botany in itself would not normally warrant our scrutiny. It was the conditions two of the bodies were found in that caused us to sit up and take notice.

'What do you think?' I ask J, but already my gut is telling me we're definitely onto something.

'Male, thirty-five years old. A geologist from China was discovered in an advanced state of desiccation,' he reads aloud. 'The other, a twenty-eight-year-old

Australian woman who specialised in botanical ethnobiology, was found in a shocking state of putrefaction. The flesh of her body, from the waist down, appeared to have been melted away, leaving the skeletal structure intact. Whilst the upper half was still recognisable and, in a state, conducive to the climate and environment it was found in.' He pauses in his disclosure, frowning.

'Both from the same party but in very different conditions.'

'Yes, it does seem very suspicious,' he agrees.

He scans the rest of the report, which adds very little else of interest as it goes on to discuss such unlikely possibilities as alien abduction and human experimentation. And with regards to the other four members of the team, no remains had yet been found. Or at least not reported. There is no photographic evidence either, so we only have our very considerable experience and intuition to go on.

'I reckon it's worth an investigation,' he concludes.

'But what do your abilities tell you?' I look at him expectantly.

'My intuition tells me that we have indeed located a remnant.'

And that's good enough for me.

'Then we've got to locate this whatever it is and eliminate it.'

'Do we?'

'You know we do. If we let this slide, then sooner or later, it's going to move into more populated areas. We're both fully aware of what these creatures are capable of. I can just nip us all over there, we tidy things up, and pop back in time for the gig.'

Yeah, right! Wishful thinking.

'Tidy things up.' He laughs and kisses me.

'Sure, it'll be fun.'

'You've got a strange sense of what entails fun. Okay, you're probably right,' he concedes.

'You know I am. It's what we do, right? Vanquish demons and slay monsters. We're good at it.'

'Okay, Van Helsing, I'm sold. When do you plan on informing the rest of the team?'

'I'll wait until we've parked up later on because first, I'm going to beat you at pontoon.'

It's the only game I ever have a hope of winning, to be honest, although he'll probably let me win — again! I'm convinced he does. You ever played cards with someone psychically endowed? It's a real bitch!

Once Deek had brought us to our destination, J and I gathered the team and revealed what we had in mind. On this occasion, it was decided that Ix would remain behind to watch over Anastassia and Deek, who would also not be accompanying us, as I was convinced our full quota wouldn't be required for what I believed would be a simple track and dispatch.

Wrong, as it turned out, but stick with me — you'll find out for yourself soon enough.

The reason I suggested Ix remain behind was because this event occurred after the incident with the tattooed arm, and I was still understandably paranoid, and if anything untoward happened as a result of this, whilst the rest of us were elsewhere, at least I could rely on Ix to take the other two someplace safe.

On this leg of our tour, we had a smaller tour bus as the roads in Europe are quite often far narrower, winding and hard to navigate, as Deek had often pointed out. No more seemingly endless miles of straight blacktop for him here as there was Stateside. The bus was equally comfortable but substantially smaller, so when I suggested portaling them back to Canada while we were in Cambodia, the offer was met with much enthusiasm from Deek.

'Och, aye. A decent bed and a shower, bring it on.'

Anastassia was less enthused, keen as she was to accompany us, but even Mist saw the sense in my arrangement, and as we planned on returning with ample time to spare so we could prepare for the gig the following night, it was agreed upon.

The three who would be taking a break in Canada — lucky them — were safely delivered. Kal and Mist taking the opportunity to pick up the tools of their trade as to have brought those weapons on tour with us would've been a border crossing nightmare.

When we arrived within the Cambodian jungle, close to the site that had been divulged on the website, it was night time.

Typical! I should have maybe thought things through a bit more thoroughly before departing. But the moon was out, which offered a little illumination, and despite the lack of sun, the heat and humidity were almost unbearable.

'A nice spot you've chosen, Alice,' Maddie commented as she flicked at some overhanging leaves and was already ossifying the insects that were homing in on our warm bodies.

I could see the tiny, and not so tiny! — insects are big here — tumbling to the ground.

Kal, on the other hand, seemed to relish the rich scent of the leaf litter and moisture-saturated atmosphere.

'There are several Angkorian sites of note within this province,' she informed us. 'In particular, the Sambor Prei Kuk.'

Quite the tour guide! Never heard of it, though.

'Is it nearby? Will we see it?' I must admit I was a little excited at the prospect.

Kal took a moment to examine the area we arrived in before answering.

I don't know whether she recognised this place or her answer was purely based on intuition.

'No,' she finally answered. 'It is several miles south of here.'

'Oh.' That was disappointing.

'Any indication of which direction we should take? Or should we await the beast tracking us down?'

'I'm not sure yet, Nikki. I'll let you know when I do.'

'There's something…' J turns around, peering into the shadows.

'I'll survey the area from above and see if I can locate anything,' Sophia offers and flits through the dense canopy, gracefully avoiding branches, vines and densely packed foliage like a hummingbird, her light slowly diffusing as she gained altitude.

I find I'm constantly swatting at the biting insects that have decided that I meet their specific nutritional requirements.

'I could try turning your skin to stone?' Maddie offers with a wicked smile.

I glower at her, but at the rate I'm being bitten, I may seriously consider her offer later on.

'Do you not notice anything unusual?' Kal asks us.

'There is a serious absence of animal life in the vicinity.' Nikki has picked up on the dearth of animal life as well.

Except biting insects!

But they're right. This nocturnal world should be alive with animal calls.

'This jungle should be teeming with life,' Kal confirms. 'But it feels deserted… abandoned.'

I pass J a worried look. It seems as if our suspicions were right.

'It is my turn to choose the next DVD to watch,' Maddie states as we await the return of Sophia.

'What! You want to discuss this right now? Here?' I can't quite believe her at times.

'I am just reminding you all. I refuse to suffer *The Greatest Showman* again.'

'I, too, find the singing Wolverine unbearable to watch,' Mist agrees. 'There is not one maiming or killing in the movie; it is shameful.'

'It was Sophia's choice,' I remind them.

'A choice she will not have available again.'

'What did you do, Mist?' J asks, sighing.

'The disc lies on the road some distance north of Athens.'

'You did not!' I can't believe their childish actions sometimes.

'Indeed, I did,' she proudly confesses.

'Nice work,' Maddie praises her.

Before I can admonish them both — I'm going to buy Sophia a new copy just to annoy them — our resident Seraphim lights her way back, enclosed within a golden sphere and descends to hover several inches above the leaf litter. Her full-length coat wafts gently around her legs, her delicate bare feet glow where they protrude from tight blue jeans. Her light wings are never in any way hindered by a jacket — they just seem to permeate the garment.

'There is a trail through the jungle just east of here. The track suggests the passage of a large animal... or creature,' she adds. 'The trail terminates on the banks of a river not far from where we currently stand.'

'Thank you, Sophia. At least we've got something to go on now,' I commend her.

Sophia then leads us through the jungle from above towards the trail she sighted, picking out the path of least resistance for us while Kal hacks back the encroaching foliage like a blue strimmer. Sophia's golden aura, although very comforting, is attracting further insects, like moths to a flame, and there are indeed a lot of moths in attendance.

And still, it's only me being bitten! Not fair.

'How come the insects aren't sucking on you?' I ask J, still peeved that they're leaving him alone.

He shrugs. 'Don't know. I've never been bothered by them.'

'They would never dare to dine on me.'

I'm not surprised, Nikki, not that anyone asked. And even the insects must sense, in an insecty kind of a way, Sophia's divinity because although they are attracted by her glow, they remain just beyond her nimbus.

'Have you tried casting a repelling spell?' Mist asks me as we stoop to navigate some low hanging vines in our path.

'Yes.' I haven't, but I didn't want to admit that it hadn't occurred to me. I give it a whirl, and my entourage of insects is pushed back. Hah! Then I slap at my neck as one penetrates my defences. Bloody things! But still, it's a big improvement.

After navigating the jungle for fifteen minutes, we reach the trail that Sophia spoke of, and it looks as if a tank has been driven through here. The trunks of the larger trees have been grazed, the bark rasped off in places, and are coated with a sticky residue, while the smaller ones lie at unnatural angles, their trunks split and broken. The smaller shrubs and saplings that have managed to secure a hold here on the jungle floor have been completely flattened. The trail itself is about fifteen to twenty feet in width, far wider than any species of indigenous wildlife, that's for sure.

J crouches down to examine the crushed remains of a small plant, his fingers coming away sticky with a glutinous substance, and he sniffs it tentatively, his head kicking back suddenly, his nose wrinkled in disgust.

'This is definitely not exuded by a natural life form,' he concludes, wiping the muck off his fingers on a nearby tree trunk.

'Like the odour that emanates from Deek's boots?' Sophia asks straight-faced.

I can't tell whether she's serious or not.

'Hah!' Maddie barks.

'The stench here is foul and more than just a result of natural decay,' Kal informs us.

I sniff the air, and I do pick up on something lingering, but Kal's sense of smell must be far superior to my own as I only detect a trace.

'What is it, Nikki?' She looks preoccupied.

'I sense the presence of more than one creature,' she almost whispers dreamily.

'You sure?' The odd persistent insect that still manages to penetrate my magic defences — how the hell do they manage that? It's something I'm going to have to work on — now pales into insignificance as I hear Nikki's pronouncement.

'I agree,' Kal confirms. 'There is definitely a pair at work here.'

'How can you tell?'

'The scent is different,' says Nikki.

'You didn't spot anything else, Sophia?' I ask. I'm getting a little anxious now.

'Just the trail we are standing on.'

'Something approaches,' Mist warns us from where she is standing, just within the forest on the opposite side of the trail from where the rest of us are gathered.

Maddie joins her, pulling her mirrored shades down the bridge of her nose with one finger in preparation.

And sure enough, I can detect something now, high in the canopy.

'Whatever it is, it's certainly not whatever made this trail,' J comments, reaching for my hand. 'It sounds too small for a start.'

'Perhaps it's the other one?'

'Perhaps.' But he doesn't sound convinced.

After a few more seconds, Maddie takes several steps into the shadows and turns to her left and angles her head upwards. How she can spot her target in that dense canopy is beyond me. But she hits her mark, and something crashes earthwards through the foliage, breaking into smaller parts as it collides with a branch before thumping into the soft earth accompanied by a flurry of leaves.

We cautiously approach to see what Maddie has dispatched.

'It is a monkey,' Nikki exclaims.

'A gibbon, actually.' J identifies the ossified remains.

'That is a monkey, is it not?'

'No, an ape,' I correct her.

'Oh, Maddie, you didn't,' Sophia exclaims, covering her mouth. 'I like monkeys.'

'A gibbon is an ape,' Nikki corrects her.

'I just told you that.'

'It was unintentional, I assure you. I merely located movement and reacted,' Maddie affirms. 'I presumed this area was clear of wildlife.' She passes the buck and stares at Kal.

'It must have been fleeing from something,' Mist surmises, examining one of the gibbon's stone arms that she has retrieved from the scattering of stone parts.

'Us?' I ask, but I feel I already know the answer to that.

'No, it was approaching us.' Maddie confirms my suspicions. 'It was more likely avoiding a predator.'

'You could collect the pieces,' Mist suggests, picking up its head. 'You could display it next to the bear.'

'No!' I'm shocked at the suggestion. 'It's in bits anyway.'

'Then perhaps you could build a rockery with the pieces.' Nikki flashes me a toothy smile.

'There is something else approaching.' Without further explanation, Sophia lifts off once again to gain a better perspective.

The Predator! Now I can't help thinking of the Schwarzenegger movie with the alien capable of blending with its jungle environment like a chameleon. I really hope it's not invisible!

'There is movement. In the canopy,' she calls down. Her flaming sword is drawn, and she uses it to point out the direction from which the creature is approaching.

'Any details?' J calls up to her.

'It's quite large… and very quick.'

What's quite large? Bullmastiff quite large, elephant-large or blue whale-large?

'Keep us informed,' I call up.

'Okay but prepare yourselves as it is approaching fast.'

Yeah, I got that.

We arrange ourselves as best we can on the side of the trail furthest from the approaching creature. The gentle rustling of leaves and the occasional creak of a branch reaching our position. For something big, it's sure not producing much noise.

Then silence.

'Sophia?'

'It has stopped, just ahead of you about thirty feet off the ground. Shall I attack?'

Nikki shakes her head.

'No, not yet,' I answer.

'I can see it,' Nikki whispers.

I peer into the shadows, but she is perfectly adapted to functioning in the dark, and I can't make anything out, but I feel J squeeze my hand; he can sense it lingering there too.

Kal slowly draws her six swords simultaneously, the honed blades singing softly as she pulls them free of their scabbards. Mist also slides her axe out of its holster, the cutting edge, glinting momentarily in the moonlight.

'What is it waiting for?' Mist whispers ahead to Nikki in frustration.

'It is watching.'

I'm as eager as I am terrified at getting this over and done with, and the thought occurs to me that this creature could be waiting for the arrival of the second monster before attacking us. So, I make a hasty decision.

'Sophia, flush it out.'

A golden beam of focused energy cuts through the canopy as Sophia commands the sword in her grasp, and it strikes the beast full-on, its unearthly screech shattering the unnatural quiet, and then I see it for the first time.

Its previous stealthy approach is now apparent as I identify hundreds of worm-like tentacles writhing across the entirety of its body. Snapping out and coiling around branches as it hauls itself forwards at an alarming rate as it barrels towards us. Its approach is so swift that I stumble backwards, and J catches my arm before I fall.

I feel J send out a psychic lance that pierces its once human mind, and it pulls itself to one side, screeching in pain. The noise it emits is painful to my ears, and I clap my hands over them as I slam it with a magical wall, and it shudders in response, faltering in its progress.

Its 'head' — if I can call it that — resembles a bud nestled within the morass of thrashing tentacles, and it swings it rapidly from side to side. Whether it's in pain or just trying to fully assess us somehow, I'm at a complete loss.

Sophia hits it again, lighting it up in all its unholy glory. Throughout the few seconds that have just played out, Maddie is petrifying those tentacles, but as soon as they snap off, they grow back with frightening rapidity.

Nikki has shadow phased and is tearing at the rear of the creature, her grasping hands forming out of the aphotic shade she has become to rip the creature apart, and in response to our formidable attack, the creature propels itself across the trail, snapping off appendages like a lizard shedding its tail as it quickly vanishes once more into the jungle like a nightmarish sea anemone, flitting from one branch to the next like the gibbon Maddie dispatched earlier.

'We should follow the beast while it is wounded,' Nikki insists, already on its trail.

Wounded! I reckon we barely scathed it, only pissed it off!

'We should split up then. We still need to follow this trail,' J insists. 'The last thing we need is the second one sneaking up on us.'

Reluctant as I am, I agree.

Nikki has already vanished from view, her shadow form allowing her to move with increased speed and dexterity.

'Okay, Maddie, Mist, stick with Nikki if you can. The rest of us will follow this trail.'

I watch on as they too vanish into the dense jungle, the look of concern very evident on my face.

'They will be fine, do not vex yourself,' Kal assures me.

'It's us I'm worried about,' I mutter. This operation was turning out to be far more than I had ever anticipated.

I later gained a pretty accurate picture of what occurred with Nikki, Maddie and Mist after discarding their heroic embellishments, of course.

I have to admit, with J close at hand, Sophia lighting the way and Kal armed to the teeth, I did feel a little comforted. But two monsters? I didn't see that one coming. Although looking back, the differing conditions the two corpses were found in was a pretty good indication. I had just assumed, as did J, that it had been the result of the same beast feeding. Maybe these two creatures had known each other in life. And death. When they had still been wholly human.

'I know Mist threw my DVD out of the window,' Sophia informs us.

'You do?' I'm surprised by her admission.

'But it is okay. I forgive her.'

'You're too good for this world,' J tells her.

'Aw, so are you, sweety.' She wraps her arms around J's shoulders and hugs him.

'Hey!'

'I love you too, Alice.' And she hugs me too.

Okay, I feel better now.

'I'd hug you too, Kal, but you're covered in swords.'

'That's okay, angel.'

Kal's the only one that calls her that without rousing a lecture about her not actually being an angel, and Sophia doesn't seem to mind. Out of everyone in our team, Sophia is the tactile one, dispensing hugs when she feels they're needed. Even to the 'grumpy twins', as she refers to Maddie and Nikki.

'I'll download the movie for you,' I promise. 'She won't be throwing the laptop out of the window.' I should have thought of that before. J downloaded *Wonder Woman* for us not long ago, and it was one of the few occasions they all sat through a film without squabbling.

The hike down to the riverbank was rather a trudge as the treads of my boots were claggy with jungle detritus, my clothes were sticking to me like clingfilm, and my bites had started to swell and itch. I was beginning to wish that I'd stayed home to keep an eye on Anastassia and Deek and let Ix come in my stead. I'm sure she would have loved this environment, one which I can attest looks far more appealing when viewed at home on the television with your feet up and a cup of hot chocolate in hand.

As Sophia had informed us, the trail did indeed terminate on the banks of a sluggish river about forty feet wide, its waters dark and ominous. Even the reflected moonlight dancing on its surface did little to dispel my apprehension as we approached.

The muddy shoreline had been churned up by a myriad of boots, made by the search party, no doubt. This was corroborated by a series of shallow depressions that had been excavated close by, the bottoms filled with murky water. And I just knew that this was where the remains of the rest of the expedition party had been discovered and exhumed.

J stood up after stooping to prise something out of the mud, its surface glinting in the moonlight. 'Cartridges,' he explained, holding it out so we could see. 'And there's a lot of them. There must have been quite a firefight here.'

Now that I looked, he was right. There were dozens of brass shells pressed into the dirt. 'Maybe they killed it?'

'Maybe,' he answered. 'But I'm getting a strong feeling that it's still here. There's no further sign of the trail continuing on the opposite bank, is there?' he asks Sophia.

'No, there was nothing else,' she confirms.

'Which suggests that this creature is fully amphibious and has probably moved further up or downstream, or...' J tails off.

'Or?' I encourage him.

'It's still here,' Kal finishes. 'The gunfire possibly drove it away. But if these two creatures are working together, in order to feed...'

'Then it was bound to return sooner or later,' I finish.

Kal nods grimly. 'A creature of the size we have established by the trail it has left would be incapable of approaching its targets with any degree of stealth. Therefore, the other creature must aid it in some way.'

As we ponder the facts and the predicament we are now faced with, I am now very aware of an unpleasant smell that seems to linger in the air. Sophia has also noticed the odour judging by her wrinkled nose, which on a Seraphim looks adorable.

J cautiously approaches the riverbank, which has been flattened into a kind of slipway, and crouches down.

'J?' I don't like where this is going.

'It's okay. We need to know where this thing is.'

'How?'

'Like this.'

He dips the fingers of both hands in the shallow water, and we all wait with bated breath. Even Sophia has come back down to earth and dimmed her aura to await the result.

J suddenly pulls his hands back, and both Sophia and I jump. Well, as Sophia is still suspended a couple of inches off the ground, she more bobs than jumps. At first, I'm convinced J's been bitten until he takes several steps back, and I can see he's still intact.

'It's right here.'

'Where?' I'm still not getting it.

He points directly to the centre of the river in front of us. 'Right there.'

'You positive?'

The look he gives me says it all.

'We need to lure it out somehow before we can launch an offensive.'

'How do you plan on doing that, Kal? I left my fishing rod at home.'

I don't fish. I don't know why I said that. This might be a good moment to deliver a classic line from *Jaws,* but right now, an appropriate one doesn't spring to mind, and I'm saving my favourite one for a more fitting occasion.

It's Sophia who amazes us all as she wades into the water. Wades? Not quite right — her aura seems to push the water aside as she drifts in. It doesn't appear as if the water is even touching her at all, which after she returned, I can confirm that it didn't — she was submerged and sealed within a protective bubble. Huh, I didn't know she could do that.

'Be ready,' she advises over her shoulder just before she disappears from view.

What do we do? I don't even know what to expect. These abominations are so monstrous and outlandish that it's impossible to predict what form they'll take or what strategies we should adopt to best defeat them. I didn't have long to consider the possibilities.

A pulse of golden light illuminated the depths that turned the silt-laden waters yellow seconds before an amorphous gastropod-like shape breached the surface like an obese manatee. Sophia shoots out of the water as if she had been shot from a cannon to avoid its sudden reaction.

Its skin was heavily wrinkled, like a thousand-year-old elephant, and mottled a greenish-brown, possibly as a result of having been partially submerged in the mud on the riverbed. I couldn't make out how it propelled itself forward as it made for the bank, but four waving appendages hung before what I can only assume to be a maw. One that looked capable of sucking the meat from bones. On three of these appendages, which were fashioned from what looked like spinal cords, were numerous bony hands grasping and clutching at the air. The fourth sprouted a head, bloated and grey, which guided that grotesque body onwards.

Why did we get the gross, smelly one to deal with? I'd have been far happier chasing the arboreal sea anemone. And take my word for it, this thing is pungent — nidorous!

I thought I'd slip in another word for the day as it does indeed smell of decaying animal matter. It is rankly odorous, to say the least.

I'm working purely on instinct now, and fighting back my nausea, I quickly pick out a handful of cartridge shells from the mud and cast a powerful spell over them as Sophia sears off one of the appendages with an intense burst of light, the bone withering and breaking. The hands still scrabble for purchase as it sinks from sight into the water.

J's also thinking fast as the blubbery monstrosity heaves itself onto the riverbank as we all retreat, exerting enough psychic pressure to pop that head like an overripe grape. The smell makes me gag, and I launch my handful of fully charged shells which deliver an electrical discharge as soon as they make contact with the beast. The crackling fingers of blue/white electricity caress its bulk, and it seems to contract in reaction to my assault, and I stoop to gather more ammunition.

Despite the loss of its head, it still thrusts its bulk further onto land, and Sophia continues to scorch its hide as I dispense another handful of charged cartridges.

Kal moves in and severs one of the other hand antennae, the blade of her sword shattering bone and sending a stream of foul green liquid spurting into the air, some of which splatters my top. I always seem to get soiled with monster gunk in these situations — typical!

Eventually, it's J that finally halts its progress, having located with his mind an organ within its mass that vaguely resembled a heart, and he crushes it to a pulp. The creature immediately grinds to a halt and deflates slightly as its volume settles, the remaining fingers on that hand appendage still attached, shuddering to a standstill.

'It smells ghastly,' Sophia comments as she flutters down to join us.

There's no denying that. It's like a sewage plant on a hot summer's day, on which someone has deposited a dead cow.

'We can't just leave it here.'

Sophia's right, and I exert a wall of energy whilst J pushes against it and shoves the creature back into the river. The view of it flattened against the invisible wall like a disgusting mutated slug-thing was a sight I'll struggle to forget for a while. Finally, it sinks from view with a noise as sickening as the very sight of it.

Kal catches the severed hand antenna that is still lying in the mud with the tip of one sword and flicks it into the river, the fingers spasming as it arcs through the air before it too disappears from view.

'One down,' J comments as the water settles.

'Two down,' states a voice from slightly behind us. It's Mist.

'When did you arrive?' I ask.

'Not long ago.' Nikki reforms out of the shadows and is joined by Maddie.

'You could have lent us a hand.'

'You had the situation under control,' Nikki surmises.

'Yes,' agrees Mist. 'Besides, the smell exuded by that one is most repellent.'

'And your own creature?' Kal enquires from where she is dipping her blades in the river to cleanse off the monster's residue before then sheathing them.

'Rubble,' Maddie confirms.

Now regarding the other team's encounter, which I will share with you, exaggerations confronted and dealt with to give you an accurate overview of what happened. Then I'm going to take a much-needed shower. Burn another top! And put some lotion on these bloody itchy bites! Perks of the job!

If I had just taken one of their narratives on trust, it would seem to you that each one of them dealt with this creature single-handedly with no aid from the other two at all. It didn't happen like that.

Nikki, being able to move far quicker than the others in her shadow form, had briskly overtaken the fleeing beast where it was still hauling itself through the canopy. Her assault, tearing out and discarding swathes of tentacles, sent it into retreat. She continued her attack, herding it back towards Maddie and Mist and steering it back down to ground level.

Once within range, Maddie and Mist began their assault, but despite Maddie's ossification and Mist hacking off those tentacles as they were extended towards her, the creature was resilient and appeared to be little fazed by the loss of its innumerable extendable mass.

It was only when that bud-like head opened, peeling back like flower petals — that's my own descriptive embellishment — to reveal the human head housed within, that an opportunity finally presented itself, or to Mist at least.

The folded back parts displayed flowing hypnotic lights on the interior surface, rather like a cuttlefish, I suggested. This generated three blank looks in return. They really need to expand their viewing horizons. But I'm sticking with cuttlefish. The shifting colours engaged to hypnotise its prey, I assumed. The head then also similarly split open and a long barb-tipped — tentacle? tongue? — lashed out. I'm thinking of that desiccated body, sucked dry of fluids.

Mist took full advantage of this 'flowering' and launched her axe with her usual precision and split it cleanly in two. Following that, Maddie's deadly stare finally took full effect as Nikki pulled the creature apart with her bare hands.

All in all, a very successful, if rather pungent — from my perspective at least — mission.

That aspect was duly pointed out by Deek upon our victorious return home as I walked past him — he was nearest me on the couch with Anastassia next to him, watching *Family Guy*. Ix had taken advantage of being back in Canada and had taken a short walk through the forest close by, not straying far in case her presence was required.

'You smell like a foosty old pair of Y-fronts and look like you've stuck your heid in a wasp's nest,' he said, leaning away from me in disgust as he caught a whiff.

Charming! I should have brought him back a souvenir. A hand and stuffed it in one of his boots one night — see if he found that funny.

But we made it to the gig in plenty of time and, to date, we haven't unearthed any other remnants. There was that other incident that happened early on during our American tour, though.

I'd stumbled across multiple reports, which spanned several months, of an inhuman spectral creature haunting some woodlands in southern Virginia. And as it wasn't far — I say far... we were travelling through California at the time, but it wasn't far for us — is anywhere come to think about it — I gathered the team one night to check out this mysterious sighting.

Well, much to my embarrassment, it turned out to be a kid in a Halloween mask. I was much more discerning in my online detective work after that. I did persuade Ix, although it took some cajoling, to 'ghost' and haunt the little shit in return. The sight of her floating skull-face flitting through the trees resulted in one very full pair of pants, and consequently, no further supernatural hauntings have been reported in that area since — funny that.

Ix's 'haunting' at least made me feel a lot better, and needless to say, Maddie found the prank highly amusing as well.